For Rox

Every story is made of a million more
Tales within tales beyond our daring minds
To know them all would be madness

The last Anvil Knight to lose his life in the Saltfrost was called Hannar. For him, surviving the hellish battle that took place there was a black shame, and the marsh showed him cruel mercy.

But that was only the *end* of his tale. There is so much more to the story of Hannar before his fall in the 'frost, though most folk don't know it. Let me tell you of the days of Golden Gar and shields of rotted pine; when dwarves dared to defy a darkness from beyond the stars.

THE
SHIELD
OF HANNAR

1

It began as so many tales do: a severed hand was floating in a mountain river. It bobbed and tumbled ghoulishly in the cold water, and its pale grasp had finally loosed the shield it once held. Nearby, that wooden disc lay partially embedded in the cool, brown clay of the bank. To whom the hand and the shield once belonged none know, for wars were many and calamities in the wild all too frequent.

What doom befell this poor soul? What shadow loomed unnoticed in the high woods? Hannar was only a dwarven boy playing in the meadows, and knew nothing of such portents. He only knew adventure, and laughter, and imagination. He jumped a narrow point in the brook, but the bluish fingers escaped his notice. He was engrossed in one of the greatest joys a young boy can know: A wooden sword.

A wooden sword is a good thing.

The cool water in Ell River bubbled along that sun-soaked day so long ago, and Hannar could not remember a better day.

And off went he, through shoulder-tall grass, over moss-covered stepping stones, and through muddy puddles spinning and jumping, but serious as stone. His quest he had forgotten, but his glare was dire and his heroism legendary.

His sword he called Spike. It was little more than a tapered branch with the bark shaved to make a grip. Quillon guards he fashioned by lashing a second stick in place with green twine, and the pommel was a smooth river rock wedged into a cracking split at the end of the hilt. Spike was as trusty as the sunrise, and smote many evil trees and weeds that day.

As the hours waned, Hannar drank from the river and found strange, sour berries to gnaw on. He ran and rolled, and grass clung to his belt. His mutterings were lost in the breeze and it was almost supper time. That was the moment, his mother calling in the distance, that he first met Wall.

Wall was lying at the river's edge, washed from some unknown forest upstream, and by fate deposited here for him, and only him, to find. It was so battered and worn to rounded corners that it looked like an ancient wagon wheel or cheese table. But through the lens of his youth and heritage Hannar saw much, much more. It was a shield. A warrior's shield.

The iron bands were wobbly and rusted, the leather belts had all but decayed to mud, and its four parallel planks had wide gaps where sand and time had perforated its might. But Hannar saw only glory. As fine a thing any dwarf could possess: A shield. His own shield.

With childish, solemn reverence he leaned forward and lifted it from the slime. It shifted and a small chunk of pine fell away, but he didn't notice. He slung the gooey belts past his hand and up his right arm, switched Spike to his left, and a wide, devilish, fanatical grin crept across his face.

No dragon could harm him now, no swamp ghouls could bite, and no Kathic scimitars would pierce his tunic. So, he whiled the evening away, soldiering and dreaming of glory and adventure in those warm summer woods.

Hannar pulled radishes and hoed rows for a week after that night. He hadn't returned home when called and missed his supper, but he slept with that soggy disc of flotsam for company. He was convinced his mother, Anna, had no idea he had found the mossy relic. It was his wondrous secret. She knew, of course, and smiled when he finally fell asleep.

"Just like his father," she whispered, both proud and sad. They were now alone at the farmhouse, for Hannar's father Hunnin was off to Duros-Tem, a willing conscript in the Iron Army. War was brewing twixt elvenkind and the dwarves of the Black Mountains, and duty was as inescapable as old age in those days.

So, they spent that summer alone together. Though they missed Hunnin and his stories, and fresh Gar from Ullgwerd and Englemoor, it was a happy time.

It is important to take notice when times are good, for doom ever lurks in this world. The memory of this summer Hannar learned to guard with the greatest ferocity, for once Hunnin returned a black shadow of death fell on The Ell Woods, and all of Alfheim. At the center of this storm of evil and wrath Hannar would stand, shield in hand, but this was only the beginning.

2

The farm lay where many did back then; perilously balanced between distant smoldering battlefields and jagged mountains. This was before The War of the Wall, or the Day of Bones, or cruel Lydea, or even the high days of Ramthas. The world was quieter back then, most of the time.

On this particular morning, though, a dim fog brooded on the hedgerows, and refused to retreat by the light of a late dawn. Hannar awoke, and wandering the house in his bare feet began foraging the pantry for goodies. His mother awoke as well but was uneasy, and tarried at the kitchen window like a worried hen.

"Where is the bacon?" Hannar sang, kissing her with a jump, transferring crumbs and jam to her cheek.

She took too long to answer. "The cupboard where it should be," she said, but kept her eyes fixed on the grassy lawn outside. Three hens wandered aimlessly amid the stubborn mist hovering there.

Hannar retrieved four strips, began eating, and hopped back to his bed. "Dragons and dark elves in the dirt! Captain Hannar is coming!"

"Your writing," Anna interrupted. He froze in his tracks. "Before any playing. Twenty lines, door shut, young man." Hannar never questioned her, but grumbled nonetheless. A micro-protest more out of habit than actual complaint. She smiled at him, he let out a sigh.

"Yes, mom," he moaned, grinning just a bit. Writing wasn't all bad; there were great stories of the Diamond Miners of Helm, and the ship builders of the Frozen Coast. Hannar shut his little door, jumped on his bed, and opened his scribner's book. The sooner it was done, the sooner he and Wall could bound into the dungeons of the back yard.

Long quiet moments passed, as they did, and he could hear his mother making tea. But then, muffled through door's planks, a thumping of boots and murmuring of voices came. Supply wagon traders from Englemoor. They came every few weeks.

There was talking, and scuffling, more thumping, and a tea cup fell. His curiosity now too much to bear, Hannar threw his little door open just as the merchants took their leave, one of them fidgeting with the clasp of his belt. His mother looked distraught, disheveled, and she was cleaning up the broken cup.

"I don't like those men," Hannar began. Anna did not chide him for interrupting his studies.

"Rice and lamb shanks for a good price..." his mother trailed off, barely finishing her statement. She gathered the broken cup, placed it on the table to repair, and slumped down in a chair. Finally, she looked over at Hannar, who was standing perplexed in the little hall. He was worried for her, but children have no words for such feelings, so they stare.

Anna giggled at last, smiled at him, and held her arms out. He ran to her and hugged her tight. She smelled like those rough road men, and he didn't like it.

"You're a fine son," she began, "the finest any mother could hope for."

"And you make good bacon!" he squirmed from her embrace, did a sort of odd monkey-roll across the kitchen, and squatted like a raccoon in the corner, munching his last piece of bacon like an animal. It made her laugh. He loved it when she laughed like that, and the strain of the rough men left her face.

She let him go to play early that day, and he picked up Spike and Wall, and went to his adventures. From bark made he greaves, and from a broad leaf a visored helm. He bumped his head, tore his tunic, and battered an evil log. From little hillocks he tumbled and into mucky tarns he fell.

Dwarven children are born tough, and sturdy against cold and hunger, but Hannar had bones like a tiger at only eleven winters old. He had a black eye most of the time, or a sprained wrist, or cuts and scratches all down one side of him. He tumbled on solid rock, jumped from waterfalls into shallow pools, and broke clumsy brambles with his chest like a battle ram. The boy was gifted with the old blood of dwarves. That is what worried his mother.

A week later, he was at it again. Wall he had repaired with twine and an old belt. It was sturdy now, and fit to his arm as if a smith had done the work. Spike he had discarded, its allure having faded in comparison. Wall was like a magic artifact on his arm. It was both weapon and guard, lever and anchor. He flipped over a broken boulder, slid through the fissure like an otter, and landed on the shield like a skiff. This way he rode down the slope to the garden, tumbling at last through a stick-pen for the goats in a heap.

He retrieved Wall, repaired the fence, and crouched in the tomatoes like a panther. A strange wagon was parked on the road beyond the yard. Muffled voices came from the house. They were back.

Hannar was suddenly no longer a soldier but a boy, and walked, arms hanging, to the front door. Dreadfully afraid and not sure why, he pushed it open and as he did, his childhood ended.

Within, in the kitchen just away from the door, the two dark-eyed road men stood. One rummaged the cupboards roughly with a sheathed dagger. He knocked jars and baskets to and fro, spilling and clanking with intentional clumsiness.

The other restrained Anna with brutal strength. He had her pinned against the counter, her tunic torn halfway off, and her skirt at her knees. She was red-faced, but no tears streaked those ruby cheeks. She saw Hannar and went pale. At that instant, the man holding her shoved her face into the wood counter, and slapped her bare thigh like a horse.

"Back to your games, whelp. We're not done 'ere," his accent was nasty and thick, cutting words up in a mess. The cupboard-rummager stopped, turned to the door, and took a step toward Hannar.

The dwarf boy was frozen solid, and petrified with both fear and uncertainty. Both men wore studded leather doublets, with square-cut black hair and curled mustaches. They were grim and dirty. He slapped her again, shoving her, and what was left of her clothes began to tear away. The rummager took one more step closer.

"Hann-"

His mother's warning was cut short by another brutal shove. Hannar's eyes burned hot, he could feel his heart pounding, but his limbs were numb as tree stumps. Wall hung from its belts in his limp grasp.

"Little bastard's goin' ta pop a vein," the rough one laughed, pushing his hips up against his mother with a thud. The closer road man realized the situation needed handling, and stepped forward again to within arm's reach of the boy, intent on subduing or even killing him.

Then something happened that had never happened before. Hannar went berserk.

3

Hokum has a charming account of dwarven berserkers. They are heralded as great warriors, fighting men, and deadly weapons of high kingdoms. In truth, they are simply madmen. This Hannar now knew as he sprang into action, throwing himself headlong into a formless rage.

His right foot he planted hard, and lurched to his left like a leopard. This placed Wall between him and the rummager. He raised the little shield, not as protection, but as a rotted wooden weapon. Reaching the window, he coiled and ricocheted toward the road man, screaming. Wall met the man's chest square, but Hannar was only a boy and slid off his braced stance in a tangle. The dirty merchant pivoted, and reached down, securing the stumbling boy with one hand and jerking him upward.

But Hannar's anger had only begun to burn. He used the jerking motion to jam his thumb into the man's crotch with horrible force, made a fist there and yanked with all his might. He was rewarded with a sickening pop as the man yelped and howled, toppling backward and grabbing his tender bits in horror. His companion saw this, threw Anna to the floor, and drew his mace from a belt loop.

When he looked back to smite the boy, the insane little dwarf was already upon him. From the counter top Hannar sprung, raising wall like a sword. The wood caught edge on the road man's cheek and tore it open, but only enough to enrage him. Hannar slid off to the side, smashing into the kitchen table in a clatter, and losing his grip on Wall.

The groin-holder regained his wits and spun, raising a boot to crush the boy. His attack missed as Hannar rolled, and he stomped splinters. From this mess Hannar grabbed one broken table leg, spun it about, braced it on one forearm, then pushed with his legs like a frog. Forward he speared into the rummager, skewering him on the jagged weapon utterly. He spat black blood and stumbled back.

Hannar was not done with him. Still flying forward, the boy wrenched the stake in its belly wound, ripped it out, and jabbed again. It stuck the rogue square in the throat, and a massive arterial spray painted the room with death. Then the second man was on Hannar's back, and hit him with the crushing metal knob of the mace. This broke ribs, and sent the boy flying like a bobber cast over a pond. He slid to a stop in one corner, seemingly dead.

"Otto? Otto, you rotter, is you dead?" the rapist prodded his ally with one boot, and holstered the mace. Anna crouched near the countertop, staring at Hannar's motionless form, but saying nothing. There was no chance of grabbing a cleaver fast enough to-

Even as she considered it, the road man slapped her hard. She spun and spit blood, and her vision went dark for a moment.

"You stay right there, love. We'll make this little visit quite worth it before I burn you and this mud hole to the-"

Hannar had regained his wits, noticed no pain, and clambered across the floor before the man could turn his attention from Anna. In a sort of sliding scissor kick Hannar crumpled into his legs, and confused him. A knotted fist retorted, snapping the boy's nose with a wet crack.

From behind Anna sprung on him now, cleaver in hand. The iron met his shoulder and hacked into hide and belt armor. He flinched, but used his weight to leverage her up and over. She caromed into the bookcase near the hearth terribly, and fell unconscious. One of her thumbs was grisly and broken where she lay.

Hannar was far from done. He jumped onto the countertop again like a feral monkey, avoiding another punch. There was a brief pause in the struggle as the road man eyed him and Hannar narrowed his mad gaze on the rogue's throat.

"Take your best shot, runt," the filthy brigand spat, "I've no qualm on putting down chil-"

Hannar didn't let him finish. Hannar didn't even hear him speak. The red hate was upon him.

Forward the stout little boy leapt, but wildly, feet first like an ape out of nightmare. The rogue batted at him, but Hannar's legs found a tangle at his doublet-belts and wrapped about his neck like a great constrictor. They both wheeled backward, and the man spun as he fell, landing on the boy with his weight. This robbed Hannar of his wind, and again the man was a fool to count the battle won. He leaned back and brushed away a mess of baskets and broken eggs.

Hannar scrambled about, gasping, and again stared the man down. His little feet were braced against the stones of the hearth, and he realized his leverage was very, very good.

"Had enough, tadpole?" The man was still mostly uninjured, and began to rise, reaching for his mace again. "I think we've 'ad enough fun today. Nighty night little bug." Hannar waited, tried to find a breath, waited. The man raised his mace for the death blow, over exaggerating as murderers often do, and Hannar shoved with all his strength against his stone footholds. Forward he flew like a lion, but his vision blurred from the pain in his chest and he missed his mark entirely, flying to one side.

In the freakish dilation of time that only deadly combatants know, Hannar saw himself flying off target and reached his left arm out desperately, latching three fingers onto the rogue's cheek bone and eye socket. His weight did the rest as he hurtled past, ripping eyeball and squirting fluid and stringy veins in a grisly mess. The man screamed, and fell, and was beaten.

The rest of Hannar's work was horrible, and fiendish, and feral. He tore the man to pieces, and pulped him with his own mace until only a mess remained. In this the boy sat down in a shocked calm, and stared into space. He slowly regained his wind, and as his tears slowed he inched over to his mother.

On her he draped a blanket, then gathered up Wall to protect her and waited there. He was soaked in blood, broken ribs and face all twisted purple and bloodied. Only those bright white eyes pierced his slimy crimson mask in the dim of the house, and he waited.

"Momma," he finally heard himself say, "Momma, wake up."

She did, eventually, and had her own swollen eye and bloody lips. One tooth she spat out, and held him without talking.

The bright summer was over, the sun-soaked grass waved no more. She held her shivering, bloodied son, and they were both in battle shock, staring blankly. Little did they know that this was but a prologue to the real doom that rolled toward them on wooden wheels.

4

South of the Black Mountains there is a wide green country called the Greenway. Beyond this, Kath and the far white shores of Aphos. On these rolling hills of lush loam fell the doom of that time, where elves and dwarves both sought to expand their lands. The Greenway was hemmed on the east by the Wall of Duros-Tem, a dwarven megalithic earthwork from times forgot. On the west side, Englemoor and the castle-states of men.

So it was that what was once a vast, silent expanse became a troubled border.

This war began as so many do, with an empty wine skin and a dare.

In the southern reaches of the Greenway stood a Fort called Friendship. Here stood the Iron Army, conscripts and militia mostly loyal to Akram and the high seat at Ramthas. These men and dwarves held no hate for the elves of Kath or even the odd toga-wearing Aphosians, and simply held the fort to stave off brigands, beasts, and bandits.

But the treaty that gave this spike-walled wooden bunker its name was ages old, and long harried by skirmishes, raiders, and unsanctioned attacks from the South. Thus, another division was eventually added to its ranks, and it held watch on the Greenway with keen eyes.

Here was posted Hunnin of Ell, Hannar's father. Watchman and second row pike was his charge, and not lightly did he mind his duty as a soldier. He had the old blood in him, and the shield-tan to prove it. His reddish beard was braided in thick knots with brass clasps, and his bunched-up eyebrows left all but dwarves to guess at his mood.

Hunnin had just finished his duties. He checked the signal fires one last time, then descended from atop the walls into the courtyard to sharpen blades, and cuff the occasional recruit as they nodded off. It was early dawn, and his relief was arriving. Forearms were clutched before eyes met, and it was Mars, an older guardsman of the fort known to shave badly and sneeze in battle.

"Fine morning, Hunn, you rat," Mars greeted him, "fend off the elves and golems yourself last night?"

"Aye," he smiled. They changed places, and Hunnin descended again to the barracks without word. The fort was quiet, but the daily regimen of training, cleanup and drills was starting to stir.

At his bunk, he shared two great mugs with Wrimm and Scratch. They offered the Gar up as soon as he entered, for to hear a dwarf sleep on an empty stomach is a terrible thing. He drank, and they had a few rounds of dice.

The Gar of Fort Friendship they brewed themselves. It was a dark, roasted stout with a bonnet of creamy foam and a hint of jerked venison. It's said that to besiege dwarves is nearly impossible, because they can live on Gar alone for months at a time.

The foam he wiped from his moustache, bade his comrades a good eve, and climbed into bed. There he made ready boots and greaves both at his bedside, into which he could jump at the sound of the Great Horn. On wooden hooks he hung his hammer, shield, and helmet. Two wooden planks formed a cross at the head of his bunk, and were adorned with cuirass, a pair of spiked pauldrons, and arming coat. Guard duty only required hauberk and vest, but it was not uncommon for a dwarven soldier to bear more than two hundred pounds of arms and armor when ready for battle.

To Udin and Thoor he made his prayers, and grumbled about a sore hip. For Hannar and Anna back home he rubbed a rune stone, and finally lay down in the modest woolen blankets. He closed his eyes and felt a wave of contentment envelope him. His conscience was clear, his duty fulfilled, his fort secure.

That was the last time he ever felt that sensation. Truly, he never could have known of the doom approaching on misty wings from the southern forest.

It began as a simple fog. The rain was heavy that morning, starting and stopping every few moments while the sun rose. The guards were wet, but resolute. For dwarves are braced by cold and damp, and find glee in the bite of winter's tooth. So, they kept their watch over spiked log tops.

Typically, the guard carried pike and shield, but Mars was somewhat of an oddity among them. Great sword only did he carry, slung over one shoulder and fully two feet longer than he was tall. The weapon was enormous, with a blade as broad as his hand and a hilt-guard carved in twisting antlers.

This great blade he named Ruin, for so it was to his foes. He planted the pommel at one boot, stiffened his back, and scanned the forest beyond the outer gate. The fog was thick indeed, like a low-floating cloud it coiled 'round tree trunks and rolled under itself as it approached on a light breeze. Eventually even the tops of the trees simply disappeared in its plume.

"Spring has conjured a real frost-fog here boys," Mars muttered under his visor. "Grey soup for breakfast."

Closer it rolled, and the rain abated briefly while mottled sun rays danced onto the clearing ahead. Mars squinted, and his hairs stood on end as he realized it wasn't fog at all, but smoke. He leaned forward, planted Ruin's squared tip in the rough wood planks beneath his feet, and listened, holding his breath. Movement. Sounds of movement in the smoke.

He scuffled three strides to his left, pulling the great blade free as he did, and leaned into a spiked wooden loophole where a longbow and quiver were mounted. He leaned Ruin on the spikes, nocked an arrow, and took aim into the smoke. Another guard noticed his action, and froze with surprise.

"Mars, what in blazes-"

But the arrow was loosed before he could finish the question. The smoke cloud was bigger than a barn and extended back into the woods beyond the limits of even Hunnin's keen eyesight. The arrow vanished into it, but impacted something with an audible thwack.

At that moment, the elven raiders erupted from their cloud like a tidal wave of steel and death.

Now elvenkind is generally perceived by most as a majestic, life-loving folk, valuing nature and beauty and immortality as guardians of good. And, for the most part, this is true. But when they make war, it is a terrifying thing indeed, for they embrace their killing fury whole heartedly, and their natural grace and talent for war make them fierce fighters.

So, they burst forth from the smoke cloud in a howl of fury. Headlong they pressed through the first gate, little more than an archway of great logs, and smashed against the fort like a storm. The gate almost gave way on their first assault; more than fifty of them all in one heave, bashing bat-shaped shields and curved kopesh swords in unison.

"To the walls!" Mars bellowed in a dwarven thunder. "The elf bastards are upon us!" He rapidly unleashed four more shafts into the attacking throng, piercing gorget and visor-slot alike with uncanny skill. For each arrow loosed, an elf perished. His kin in kind joined the fray, and soon dwarven shafts began skewering the hoard with terrible effect.

Mars dropped the bow and darted to the gate-watch, bringing up Ruin above him like a war banner. To this shining silver blade the guard rallied, and like beetles they bunched and gathered behind the gate.

"Brace!" Mars yelled at them, and they did. Locking elbows and digging booted toes in their shields formed a bulwark of steel, and they pressed inward. Mars noticed Hunnin in formation, tunic, trousers, and boots only, and gritting his teeth.

The elves tried again, leaping and hacking at the gate like grasshoppers gone mad. The treaty was ended, the skirmishing over. This was an attack intended to wipe the fort off the map.

5

The dress would not fit.

All the whale bones in the Black Ocean couldn't squeeze her into the damned thing, no matter how hard the chamber maid tugged and cursed. She tied the bodice anyway, with mere nubs of string remaining, and sewed buttons to the back with string frogs to loosen the shoulders.

It was hideous. A frilly, ruffled, green-striped monstrosity intended to arouse men and keep women from breathing. Gods forbid a woman should be relieved of light-headedness for even a moment, lest she topple all the warring world of Lords and Kings in one sentence.

The mirror, with one odd ripple in it that elongated her left leg, yawned at her. She could not muster a smile, and the doom of appearing in court as some kind of sex-trophy dawned on her in waves of anger.

"Would Miss like a sip of chilled Gar to ease her nerves? Court *can* be a trial at times," the maid murmured, keeping her gaze downward.

"I'm no lady or duchess, Wenn," the mirror-gazer replied. "We will speak plainly together. Let's both have a mug, for pity's sake." They sat. One sipped, one gulped.

Her name was still Elisa back then, before her grim nickname took its place. For that day was a doom long in the making: A wedding meant to tie the men of Englemoor and the hill tribes of the Nurin foothills. And of all who would benefit, Elisa's Uncle, Siris, stood chief among them. She was being pawned like a donkey at market.

In truth, Elisa never intended to go through with it. Hers were the hill folk, and her blood mighty. With a hundred spears outside her chambers she had passed the days, unable to fathom a means of escape. And so, she found herself here, stuffed like a supper pig ready for slaughter.

She quaffed another mug, and her choler settled.

A sharp knock at the door and the farce was unfolding. Two hundred leather-capped subjects had gathered in Englemoor square. There was an air of cautious celebration, but the taverns were brimming and the sewers more so. On the raised stage stood Uncle Siris, a bearded colossus of a man. He had married into her family from the Grey Road clans years ago. The groom-to-be also there stood, sweating and looking peckish as a starved goose. Elisa had forgotten his name. With them stood a division of armored pikemen, and, most notably, a headsman at the ready. The latter was hooded, and leaned on his grim, ten-foot chopper with dark menace. Lutes and laughter bubbled on the stone pave.

"Gentlefolk and ladies of Englemoor!" a crisp, bright tenor voice cut the din. "Draw your attention to the stage, and prepare to witness peace in the forging!" Folk gathered, and shuffled forward. The only space they left was near the headsman, who reeked of dried blood.

"Ah yes, yes," the crier continued. He was a spry, tiny fellow in green and yellow pantaloons with waist tassets and a three-buckled rapier frog. He popped and lunged as he spoke, and knew his craft well. "Greetings all, and morrow good met!" From thin air, he produced a goblet, guzzled its red contents in one spectacular pour, flipped it, spun it, and the silver cup landed impossibly back in its waist loop. The crowd cheered, and one drunk fell over.

"Be on with it, clown!" Siris bellowed. He sat in a great wooden chair with lion hand rests, but was visibly uneasy. The man was unimpressive, despite the relative grandeur of the throne, and greed dripped from his mustache.

"Indeed, Siris of Nurin's folk! On with the wedding!" the bard spun to the far side of the stage, wowing the crowd again. "Let all here witness the rightful joining of Elisa Fenn's daughter, and Barille of Westerfund, duke of that fine land and heir to Fort Spear! By these bonds we make peace with the folk of the Nurin hills, and bind an alliance against the weird and the wicked! Who here say otherwise?"

There was an odd quiet, as at all weddings and such moments. At last one voice cracked the pause. Folk flinched.

"Blast this slavery to the hells!" boomed Elisa, her voice deep and rusty like a bear waking from sleep too soon. Her handlers yanked her back by her shoulders, and finding her far stronger than they expected, one bound her hands with leather thongs and jerked her into line. At this smiled Siris, and the groom looked terrified.

The mockery continued until the two of them stood before all. Elisa's rage was boiling, and poor Barille wanted no part of her wrath. At last the kiss was announced, and when Elisa turned away from that slimy pale lord, Siris jumped from his stool like a tiger. One of her shoulders he pushed back, and with his other, gauntlet-clad hand he cuffed her. The steel rings opened her lip, and filled her mouth with blood. His intent was to quell her rebellious spirit, but instead he ignited that savage fire that made her people fierce, and she had enough of peace.

Instead of returning the cowardly slap, she faced the crowd, and spat blood. Her hands she raised, and tore the leather ties at her wrists like paper. With one inhale she flexed her back like a panther, and her dress split in two. The bodice cracked like a chicken's neck, and she ripped the frilly bell from her waist all in one furious rage. Bare she stood before them all, save a beige linen strap across her chest which impossibly contained her bosom, and a waist-string with two loin cloths for modesty.

A gasp went through the mob. She was built like a siege machine. Her massive shoulders and biceps shocked the men and made the women proud, her thighs were like ivory tree trunks, and she cracked her knuckles like a pit fighter ready to die. Around each fist she twirled shreds of white cotton from the dress. She was tall, and grim, and made the groom seem like a matchstick.

The spearmen strode forward, but before they could surround or restrain, she was upon them like a cornered animal.

On the ball of her left foot, now bare, she spun and ducked. A spear tip gouged her shoulder like hot wax, but the fury was on her, and she felt nothing. Instead she caught the oak haft with her right hand, planted her right foot like a sprinter, then clinched down in discus pose. The haft cracked, and the armor-clad man was flung bodily from the stage. The crowd gasped with shock.

Siris, a hillman himself, was barely surprised. This very outcome was the reason for the presence of the headsman. For to defy a righteous union was a death sentence for a woman in those times, and the dowry would be paid, regardless, as damages. He grinned, and nodded to his hooded henchman.

More spears, sweeping and jabbing at her. She sprung forward, and rammed two scale-clad guards with a thud. The both pitched backward, and had not even hit the ground before she had skewered another with his own weapon. Only two more men-at-arms remained. One bolted, wetting his breeches, and the other made a feeble thrust from his shield's safety. Elisa evaded the spear point, gladly absorbing a small cut to the ribs, and ripped the shield from his hand, breaking his arm. He bent over and squealed like a child stuck in a well.

Strapping the cowering guard's shield to her arm, Elisa turned to the crowd and scanned for threats, her eyes black with battle. Only one foe remained as her Uncle watched, slowly backing away: The Headsman.

He was clad in ring mail skirt, thigh boots, and was shirtless save a leather frog that crossed his mighty chest. He was not muscular, but a corpulent giant. A head higher than Elisa stood that tattooed killer, and bent his hooded head to target her throat. At his side the grim thing stood blade-down. The axe was black-bladed, ragged, and massive. The iron haft alone must have weighed eight stone, and it stood ten feet from point to pommel.

With a grunt, he twirled the mighty weapon to bear, and aloft it went. Elisa leaned back into her left foot, bracing, for there was no avoiding this. Her only concern now was finishing this quickly. The full city guard would be here in moments. She had to dispatch this titanic fiend, and be off to savage freedom and law defied.

The blade came whooshing down with a rushing of mass. The crowd was dispersing now, terrified. Elisa did not absorb the blow, but angled her steel buckler to simply divert the force. Even so, the thing was huge, and split her shield like bread. Her arm she withdrew in the nick of time, and the axe met the stage with a crack. The shield was pinned there with it, almost hewn in two.

"Stand still, girl!" the Headsman bellowed in gurgling baritone. She did not comply, but pushed into the weighted foot. Her thighs strained like a war horse, and with one hooked elbow she caught the axe haft as the Headsman struggled to free it. Planks splintered and flew, but as the shards of hickory drifted around her, she caught her own wrist, and twisted with terrible strength.

The Headsman was no easy wrestling partner though. He leaned back against her wrenching, both arms popping and bulging with sweat and strain. Their eyes met and time stopped. It was like a wooly mammoth and a sabre tooth in ancient primordial battle: both unstoppable, both refusing to back down.

In battles such as these, when history depicts a great draw for all to witness true prowess, one factor decides the victor: Righteousness. The foe who has nothing to lose, nothing to fear, and the truth as her armor will always prevail when all else is even. So it was this day.

She met his glance, managed a tiny smile, and she was beautiful. Her high cheekbones glistened with blood, and her lovely blonde locks whipped in arcs and waves. Her might was her beauty, and with that she was well endowed. The gods had made her strong, and the time to hide it had passed.

She realized she had the upper hand, compressed her stomach, and the axe came free. The force of it gave the headsman the slightest stumble to his heels, and it was all she needed. In one horrible extension, Elisa spun the weapon above her head. On her toes she ascended, and like a marble statue of the glory of youth and power she brought all her noble blood to this second. The axe descended, and a hooded head rolled across the wooden stage to the horror of all.

Siris took another step backward, now afraid of her. The axe in both hands she leaned back and flexed her chest with the hot rush of victory. Those who saw it will never forget that look, those eyes.

But the glory of this grim day was not hers to relish, for the guard revealed itself at the court's far corner. On one shoulder, she slung the hellish blade, and bound away into the hamlet streets beyond. Rounding a corner, she dragged that great weapon into the dim, overflowing sewers and vanished.

She was bleeding terribly, and in need of a plan. One wrong move, and she would be tortured to death as an example to all.

Even there, in her dank, fuming hiding hole among the filth, the blood and the rats did not bother her. She was a free woman, and by her own hands. Her kin had brought her up well, and her father would be proud if he were alive. Her mother she never knew, but closed her eyes and visualized a face anyway.

"I am Elisa no more," she whispered in the black, wiping the blood from the great broad blade, "Let them call me the Headsman."

6

The gate was shattered, the wall crawling with kopesh-swinging elves, and that awful smoke cloud curled and encroached like a giant grey squid. Long, deep boot gouges tracked the inner gate where the dwarves had been pushed. The battle now raged on in the center courtyard of the fort. Small fires broke out here and there, and those stout defenders fought for their lives like wolves cornered in a canyon.

Two dozen of their number lay slain at the elves' boots. Mars and Hunnin, Wrimm and Scratch still stood shoulder to shoulder, hacking and bracing and shoving. Hunnin was covered in blood, as he had no armor fitted. Half his great beard was torn out, now clutched in the pale dead hand of some elven murderer.

And murder it was, for this troop was no elven army, or royal cadre. They were avengers driven by the rage of some hateful rebel. Their armor was not uniform, and their fighting style was wild and bloodthirsty. This was not war, this was savagery.

"They've got us on our heels, boys!" Mars yelled, knocking a sword aside with Ruin and returning the attack tenfold. "A plan would be fantastic."

Wrimm leaned to one side, caught a kopesh slash in the ribs, broke the blade with one gloved hand, and crushed the attacker's skull like a pumpkin. "Something drives these poor wretches forward! Their fury is reckless, and I'm hungry as an ox!"

The dwarves laughed. It was not a laugh of mirth or even humor, but a form of battle cry. When war was upon them their courage was unbroken, even as their kin died stick-straight, or flying through mid-air like champions in the arena.

"Have a look, Wrimm! We'll hold the damn stairs," Hunnin bellowed, shoving two spear thrusts back. The elven attackers were enraged, and redoubled their effort. One spear pierced clean through the dwarven wall and into Hunnin's shoulder. He howled with anger, "That's my mug arm, you filthy waif!" With his shield arm, still mostly unhurt, he extended upward, then down in a wide arc. The heavy shield snapped the spear like a twig, and pitched its wielder forward, setting him face to face with Hunnin. Though far shorter, Hunnin's mighty skull was twice the mass of that point-eared ranger, and he head-butted the lovely face into a red ending.

Wrimm took his position above, scanned the battle, and made report. "They swarm and swirl like locusts," he started, "Some captain is at their fore, there by the silos across the courtyard. He is a robed figure, all in red, but the smoke is relentless!"

"What of Kuro, and Ol' Jeb?" Mars yelled back, "Still in the fight?"

Wrimm swallowed, tightened his grip on his hammer, "Fallen..." he muttered. Their captain had died, two elven throats in his broad hands. "There are too many of them!"

"Too many for what," Hunnin laughed, "a bloody tea party?" With that, he ended his opponents, and the splash of elven blood gave him an epiphany. "Come on, gents, let's be cowards!"

Now it is important to note here that dwarven humor can be quite dry, especially when facing certain death. But there is an unspoken understanding between their kind that courage will never falter. Their trust in one another is intrinsic, their loyalty like the air in their lungs. So, the three fighters took Hunnin's cue without question, and followed when he darted from combat into the nearby smith's hut.

In one fast motion, back threw Hunnin a great heavy rug, and below it a hatch was yanked open. In went all four dwarves, clanging and banging like steel beetles. This tunnel all of Fort Friendship knew, it led out to the well for use in siege situations. They raced down its shadowy narrow.

The battle pressed inward, into the fort. The elves had a terrible momentum, and now and again returned to their captain's post, and as they did, seemed rejuvenated or bolstered, then re-entered the fray with murderous fury renewed. It was an odd, magical thing. The worst kind of magical thing.

Several elves saw Hunnin and his company flee into the hut, and paid no heed. "Cowards," they assumed, and continued the killing. This was the elven hubris at work that would spell their undoing decades later at Duros-Tem, where the Falcon king laid their people low with valor true. Hunnin was counting on this hubris, and his gamble paid off.

The four dwarves found themselves outside the fort gate, rushing in on the elven rear ranks. The fools had trapped themselves. The stout fighters waded into their enemy and hewed them like wheat. They began to scatter, but Wrimm held fast the gate bar, and swung it down with a bang. Now they were penned in, being destroyed from three sides, and the tide turned.

But it mattered not, for this company of elves drew its strength from the black dimensions beyond the mortal world.

Their captain turned to this new threat, Mars at its lead swinging Ruin like a figure from a mythic tapestry. From the red robes and ring mail of the elven champion, a long, thin hand emerged and revealed an object. It was glowing and prismatic, a thrumming thing with sharp, ragged edges like stone plucked from the deep earth. The air grew hot as brimstone and the eyes of the elven ragers glowed like coals.

"Devilry!" Scratch yelled. Scratch never spoke, and the call jarred every dwarf there.

And devilry it was.

Hunnin again proved his great worth and wit, for instead of hacking and smashing at the soldiers, he darted to one foot, then the other, spun and dove forward like a sprinter. At the captain's door was he in an instant, and the elven soldiers all turned, shocked and threatened by the maneuver.

His kin made good on the opening, and crushed the burnished cuirass of every elf that drew breath. But as Hunnin lifted his weapon and strained to land one mighty attack on that artifact-wielding demon, a great red bolt of lightning arced in the smoke with a deafening crack of thunder.

Every combatant fell like a twig in the din. Hunnin was struck square in the forehead with the bolt, blowing what hair remained into oblivion, scorching him, and leaving a gaping hole near his neck, where his thick shoulder muscles sizzled and went slack.

"Hunnin!" Mars howled. He scrabbled to his boots, lurched forward, and grabbed Hunnin by the shirt. Wrimm and Scratch hurled their hammers in unison, striking the weird robed figure squarely, but he was unhurt.

Then it happened. A dead elf gained his feet, shook the dizzy of death from his crimson-stained eyes, and renewed the fight. Then another. The dwarves were outmatched, and wise enough in war to know.

The four of them bunched up with the other half-dozen survivors still fighting, backed to one end of the court, and bashed through the log wall to make an egress. The fighting never stopped, Hunnin was barely breathing. The bitter, metallic taste of defeat came to Mars' throat, and they darted into the woods to disappear.

That was how the War of the Wall began. And, not many know it is so, but Hunnin, father of Hannar, was the first dwarf ever to lay eyes on the creature that would one day be known as Red Fang.

7

The air in the woods that morning was low and warm, drifting up from the seething heat of Kath. The dwarves of Fort Friendship huddled in a hollow together, stealing a few moments rest before the elves were upon them again.

Hunnin was wounded terribly and would not survive much more running, so the fight was inevitable. As Wrimm opened his eyes, he saw Scratch at the watch, and Mars doing one-armed pushups on a nearby boulder. This gave Wrimm a warmth, for he knew the courage of dwarves would never break, even under the strain of a thousand years. Their tales would be legends, and they could walk among the gods without shame.

"It's a good day," Mars said, breaking the forest quiet and standing up, "A good, warm day to fight. Scratch old boy, surely you've a scrap of bacon and tomatoes in that satchel of yours."

Scratch grinned wide, revealed his traveler's cache, and started a tiny fire.

"Don't be shy," Mars continued, hopping down and walking over to them, "Let the devils see us! Let them ambush or jump down from trees or hurl bloody magical porcupines at us! Blasted liars and murderers every one! Let them come! But not before breakfast, by Udin!"

To this the survivors gave a grumble and a cheer, and one of them hopped up from his hidey hole. His name was Brann, and though new to the fort, he'd already proven his worth a dozen times over. He was clad in a ring mail skirt and a smith's belt only. His bare dwarven feet were like clubs all covered in earth and moss, and his blonde beard was stained red from the battle. No weapons or armor or shield had he, but his chest was broad, and his breath deep, and his eyes held fury undimmed.

"It's Hunnin we fight for," he said with a bright tone, "We slay them all and make for the farms of Ell valley. There we mend our man-at-arms, and get word to King Akram of this treachery."

Mars nodded.

The rest of the dwarves, ten in all, stood and helped with the cooking. They tossed each other strips of bacon, balanced fried tomatoes on their noses, and guzzled their last skin of stout. It was a merry breakfast, save for Hunnin's slumped form, wrapped in a smith's apron. Still breathing, he lay unconscious, that hideous wound at his skull and neck gaping but bloodless.

"Brann, why not let our guests know breakfast is concluded." Mars cracked his knuckles, belted in his cuirass and helm with silent routine, and took deep breaths through his great broad nose. It was a very good day to fight.

The other dwarves followed, hefting up shield and spear alike, and forming an impromptu phalanx in the hollow without words. Scratch stomped Wrimm's toes for fun, and they smacked and picked at each other like bored children.

Stashed they Hunnin's limp form in root's shadow nearby, safe and sound, with a hot slab of bacon near his nostrils to make his deadly dreams good and bright.

"Oy you pale cowards!" Brann yelled, but in a sing song tone that mocked the elves with dwarven mirth unmatched, "Why not pop out your hidey holes and die good deaths here with us? Mars has done enough pushups for all of us, so there's no need for a warmup!"

The company chuckled and mocked his oratory skills.

"Besides, you pale little liars, I've no weapon nor steel skin to stop you, come on out and give ol' Brann a fight to remember, eh?"

There was a long quiet, and the wind in the treetops rushed and abated in strange rhythms. If one twig snapped at that moment, battle would be joined, but no sound defied the grim nothing.

Finally, a low, unnatural voice broke the moment.

"Brann Goor's son," the voice hissed from the rocks at the hollow's southern edge. "You crave death so eagerly for one so young?" The voice belonged to the red-robed captain of the elven legion, who then revealed himself among the boulders. The dwarves tensed on their toes, but none sprung, for the captain was well beyond five strides. They were ready to fight, but not fools.

"Get on with it, wizard," Mars answered, swinging his immense great sword down from his shoulder, one hand on hilt and one clutching leather-wrapped blade.

"Yes, yes, you rude little ape," the captain's words returned from a black hood shadow. "Curious, how impish little savages like you have repelled my kin over the years. But I have overcome the weakness and false mercy that has kept our superiority at bay, wretch. I am your slaughter, yet your foreheads are too thick even to be afraid."

Brann bent to one side, lifted a fist-sized pebble, and before anyone even noticed, hurled it directly at the captain's head. It met its mark with a whack, knocking the hood back. The captain was an elf, normal enough, save a pale, veiny look to his hairless head. He was thick-muscled and had the jaw of a fighting man, but the deep temples and forehead of a scribner or magician. The rock left a great red welt on one brow.

The dwarves broke into raucous laughter, and the captain trembled with rage. From the stones nearby arose the legion of elves, their number somehow undiminished from the previous battle. They were at least fifty strong, and though many bore the wounds from the battle at the fort, they moved as if unhindered by them.

"You didn't bring enough men!" Brann bragged, putting his fists up like an old-time ring fighter.

The anger left the captain's face, and again he withdrew that odd-looking object from the sleeve of his robe. It was sort of crystal or fragment of flouritic rock. It vibrated as he muttered some black spell, but dwarves are not known for a fear of anything, least of all spells and magic.

The words ended as the dwarves leaned into fighting stances, and at the instant the tension became unbearable, Mars sprang into action as the spell was unleashed.

What happened then was a thing of terror: A story that was told and retold for centuries to frighten children and bolster warriors' hearts.

8

Elisa, the Headsman, the deadly bride of Englemoor, was laid low. In the black tar of those city tunnels she lost her wits, and fell to her wounds to bleed in the muck. Only her hill-blood, forged through hard living in the cold and the hunger of the North, kept her alive.

It seemed a life age she languished in the bowels of the city. Day and night became one, long feverish madness. The tunnels yawned and twisted when she fled angry voices above, and rats skittered on her when she slept. Her dreams were black, and in those rare moments of lucidity she enjoyed, she wondered if her arranged marriage would have been so bad as to choose this life instead.

But, that choice was well behind her. She was a symbol now, an example of female defiance, of freedom, of strength. There was no going back. The yoke that women had endured was generations old, and it would not be cast aside easily. And so she endured, and healed, and her intentions grew dark and unnatural.

History has faded how long she festered in that dark hell, for stories this old lose their corners in places. The business of Englemoor went on. It was believed she died somewhere below, alone. This fate gave a convenient ending to the Bloody Bride story. Men who beat their wives had nothing to fear as long they thought her gone.

When her wounds at last were closed, and scars formed, it was near the day the elves took Fort Friendship. But the folk of Englemoor knew nothing of elven treachery, save Elisa, who discovered the beginning of a coming storm.

It was morning. She was free from fever, and rested, and fed on found scraps. Her mind never truly returned to normal, though, and she prowled the dark like a serpent. She had to escape the city and feel sunlight again or she might lose her mind completely.

That is when she saw the first of them. A dark blur slid through a grated sun ray in the gloom, when the town was still asleep. It was a slurping, wet, rubbery thing. Called from some elder dimension by elven blasphemy, for no other race had magicks as they possessed. The tentacled mass was etched in elven writing and bulging blue veins. Barbed suckers accentuated the horror.

"You're in my home, wretch," Elisa muttered. Her voice was hoarse and low; she had changed. "What treacherous plot brings you here?"

The thing seemed to hear her odd banter, for in gloom's shadow it coiled, and paused, then sprung like a cobra.

Its mass was deceptive. The fat, blobby body was four stone at least, and barreled into Elisa like an iron cauldron. She braced with one foot back, catching the whipping coils with both massive hands and straining to hold her ground. It wrapped, and constricted, and the suckers burned her flesh with acidic spit and tiny hooked teeth.

"Gods!" she burped, stumbling back. The headsman's axe, a massive thing that barely fit upright in the tunnels, was just out of reach. So was the eye-holed hood she had made her own grim death's mask. It was a contest of her bare hands and the monster's lashes.

A third tentacle came from nowhere, swinging around like a scorpion's tail. It wrapped solidly about her head, blinding her and burning her horribly. She spun like a wrestler, slamming into the wet pavers below with terrible force. One rubbery whip burst under her enormous weight, and blue ichor splashed onto the moss, burning it into grey smoke.

In a feat of strength beyond most, Elisa pushed upward with one arm, separating the whip from her face and pinning the monster to the ground. Her lower hand she made into a terrible fist, squeezing acid blood from the thing like an untied hogwurst. She extended her upper hand, spreading her mighty shoulders, and her muscles bulged and popped like a draught horse. The thing was torn utterly in two.

She flopped to the wet stones and tenderly touched the burns across her head and face. In a drain's pool, she saw herself and knew that what beauty she once had was truly gone. She saw only a monster. That reflection drove her pushed her closer to madness than any tenure in the sewers or nights in black fever. It occurred to her, there in the depths, that to think one's self a monster is the first step to becoming one.

She steeled her emotions, and stood. In hood's shadow her eyes fumed, and she lifted the axe with grim purpose.

Stepping over the ruined beast she took pause. In the tunnel beyond, just now revealed in dawn's glow, a sight from nightmare unfolded.

Thousands of them. They piled and whipped and tangled like a bed of breeding snakes. Wet slurping and rubbery slaps punctuated the hellish visions of their brood. It was a mass as high as a man and thrice as wide, like a ball of ropes all knotting and probing and twitching with slime-skinned death.

So, she ran. She did not stop until she reached the river drains, and sunlight renewed on Launder's Rock. From that small crag, she could see Englemoor laid out, and like a weird colossus she stood motionless in the sun surveying her past. Death stalked them all.

Would she remain, and be their hated savior and herald of doom, or take to the road's foot and become a wraith of the wild? Though her look was a terror to behold, and her mind a black pit of confusion and determination, she was not evil, and the decision came to her easily. There was no leaving. Englemoor was the target of some dark spell, and spells make nauseous the hill folk.

She stooped in her hellish hood, leaned the axe, and washed the filth from her fists. The sun climbed, and on golden skin those warm rays renewed her.

"They'll not listen to a murderer," she mumbled, tightening her ragged wraps, and rubbing one sore shoulder. She looked long at that hooded face in the water. "The Headsman will draw them out, and we'll crush these poisonous demons together.

"Fight alongside your accusers?" some new voice echoed in her mind.

"At least expose the threat," she returned. "Then it's to the road. I've enough of towns and tunnels."

She stood, tall with new purpose. Hers was an exquisite form of ferocity, like an avatar of ancient bloodlines in the Age of Titans. She rested one hand on her chest, a rare and feminine gesture. She was still a woman after all. Some wisp of an old dream danced at the edge of her shadowy mind, but she could not place it. Her softer side was truly dead.

The hand fell from its delicate perch at her bosom and wrapped 'round the great axe like a claw. The knuckles cracked and the leather haft creaked. The sun climbed higher. It was a good day to fight.

9

Every dwarf tells the story a little differently. Only one thing is certain in history's bleary eye: the dwarves fell that day. And, as if their utter defeat wasn't enough, a doom of ages befell that simple smiling dwarf called Brann.

As the red-caped captain revealed his other-worldly object with menace, the company of elves beside him lurched forward. They were pale and dirty from the morning's killing, and ready for more. Most of them sported hideous wounds or spatters of their own blood. Their armor had that curved, fluted look that heightened their woe, each crowned with a bladed cheek-helm and black horsehair tassel. One had but a single arm remaining to carry his kopesh into the battle. How were they even standing?

Again, the tiny obelisk in the captain's hand thrummed with evil. Mars sprang from Brann's left side, his broad two-handed blade rising above and behind him. For a dwarf, he covered tremendous distance in one leap, and placed himself squarely twixt both forces. Hunnin was still well-stowed and unnoticed, Wrimm and Scratch drew their axes and set their toes.

Brann, however, was frozen. His eyes turned milky white and from sockets bulged like ripe snowberries. His hands were contorted into claws at his sides, and he dropped his shield like a wooden dummy. This Mars did not see, for he was up to his beard in whizzing kopesh blades and dagger swipes. Eight elves fought he all at once, and when Wrimm and the others joined the fray it was a sight to behold.

Dwarves always fight in a chevron formation. They fall in elbow to elbow, the mightiest at the point, and with each half step forward they lower their heads and attack in terrible unison. It is a sight that must be beheld to truly appreciate its martial efficiency.

Ahead of the forming chevron, Mars beheaded the two fastest elven attackers. Before they could even slump to the moss, he had spun in a follow through, letting the weight of Ruin carry him around. There he met another warrior square in the chest, and the blade sank beyond seeing into the ringed armor like a cleaver. There Mars let the blade rest, braced on its mighty hilt like a ship's cleat, and used the leverage to kick his next target upside the ears.

The whole mess of them fell in a clatter, and the sword came loose in a terrible spray of red. Three more pale attackers leapt over this scene and smashed into Wrimm and Scratch, who led the other dwarves in tight defensive formation. There was redeemed a thousand years of dwarven tactical thinking and training, for the elves broke on them like clouds on a mountain. Axes whirled and dwarven steel met elven teeth with a crunch. The tide of the battle quickly turned.

Yet another wave of elves met their end, but with them went Wrimm. His death has been told in so many tales, it's hard to know what truly happened, but this remains clear; he died stick straight and standing, no less than two curved elvish blades scissoring him all but in two. Eyes open and still showing teeth, he went rigid, and let fly a cry so terrible those few dwarves who yet stood shuddered, and were driven mad with battle fury.

Mars waded through them like grass, cutting elves in whooshing swings and taking iron-booted strides with each deadly arc. Scratch had lost all his allies, those brave dwarves of Fort Friendship, and stood alone atop a great broad root at the battle's edge. He threw one attacker bodily across the clearing in a shocking feat of strength, lifting the elf by his upper jaw with bloody fingers. But then he, too found death on elvish steel, and fell backward into a hollow. Folk say a thick green heather grows over that place now, and goodly spirit folk gather each moonfall to sing a great dirge for the hero that sleeps there.

Now Mars and Brann alone remained alive, save unconscious Hunnin is his hidey hole, and fewer than ten elves still fought. There was the briefest moment for Mars to look back, and squint the blood from his eyes. He saw Brann, and the warmth drained from his hands in fear. To say this is no small thing, for this was the greatest warrior of that time and place, and he feared nothing.

Brann convulsed, and sweated terribly, his eye sockets sunken and grey. Into the sky he stared like a corpse, and his mouth gaped with slack mumbling. Lumps and coiling shapes moved and twisted beneath his skin, and his chainmail swayed with his suffering. The hum of the Red Captain's artifact grew unbearable, and suddenly Brann's gaze cleared. He looked squarely at Mars.

"I am Brann Gulgynn," he began in a dead, lifeless tone. It wasn't truly his voice. "I am the son of Goor, and brother to Mars. In Hammer Peak's cradle was I reared, and at Fort Friendship made honorable. All these things I am, and more..." he trailed off, staring directly into Mars' eyes, who stood transfixed in terror.

At that moment, the forest sounds silenced, the humming stopped, the very air froze in place, and Brann Gulgynn was torn apart.

From his mouth sprang a trio of blood-wet tentacles, lined with barbed suckers and whipping back on themselves as the dwarf's teeth scattered onto the pine-carpeted ground. His arms split in two like plank wood, and from those awful stumps more of the writhing whips unfurled. To one knee he stumbled, as his left boot split to shreds revealing a fatter, goo-slimed trunk of rubbery muscle. It was a horror beyond sanity, but Mars held his ground, and his grip on that massive blade tightened.

"Behold," the Red Captain howled, pocketing the artifact once again and raising his arms like a preacher, "the power of the elves!" At this, Brann, or what was once Brann, let loose an echoing scream. It was deep and hoarse, and bloody, and in his torn throat gurgled with death.

Mars said nothing. He curled his toes in his boots, breathed in, and in his heart called on Udin to grant him strength. He had none. His knees would not budge. A glance revealed the

Red Captain had gone, with what remained of his company, leaving the corpses of their kin to rot.

Brann continued his awful transformation, growing and splitting and tearing into ribbons of blood. The tentacles multiplied impossibly, erupting and tumbling all around the clearing. They wrapped 'round tree trunks and upturned noble old stones. In an instant they would be at Mars' feet. He had to act.

Now dwarven gods are not known for their attentive nature. Udin least of all, who sits in dark judgment on a throne of storms. They are cold, aloof beings of stone and silver whose gaze remains on the fathomless reaches of time, not the squabblings of mortals. But that red day was different, and once again Mars called upon his gods from his heart. He bade them forgive him, for he was to cut down his own brother in arms. He was not only to see this abomination, but to wade into it, and know the hot hell of a friend's blood soaking.

That day the gods answered. Udin himself reached down from between the very stars and touched Mars' shoulder with one great finger. This thing the dwarf knew in his soul, and with iron tears he set one boot to solid earth, and twisted the hilt of his great sword with creaking knuckles. The first swing was the hardest, and lopped a waist-thick tentacle in twain like paper.

Black, purplish gore spewed like a geyser. The Brann-thing whirled, and the whips combined their purpose. They lashed terribly, and coiled overhead to strike like cobras. But Mars had the fury of old thunder on his brow, and was unstoppable. He strode forward, dragging barbed suckers with his mighty thighs, and with three flowing cuts he hacked his way to face his brother.

Up close, what remained of Brann was even more terrible. His jaw was dislocated, one eye had burst entirely from its socket, and half his helm had split open to reveal a pack of tangled squidlings whose hungry suckers twitched and devoured bits of brain.

He paused not. Mars Guernee Gulgynn let his blade twirl to one hip, reversed his two-handed grip, and in a tremendous feat of strength executed an upward swing no human could ever dream of performing. Six feet of steel sung in the morning dew, and threw a moon-shaped arc of purple mist. From knee to neck was Brann hewn utterly, and the two hellish halves slid apart.

But it was far from over.

The dwarf gone, only the horrors remained. They burst from his split rib cage like eels from a dead whale, growing and grabbing and tearing in every direction with senseless malice. These abominations did not please Udin, and his blessing upon Mars continued.

There, alone, in that clearing of pines near the smoking ruin of Fort Friendship, Mars fought them. He cut them, stomped them, tore them from their roots, and laid low every last writhing one of them. He was covered in filth, wracked by a thousand torn cuts and gaping bites. His armor was split and his nose broken. One hand sported three broken fingers, broken buckles and stray chain rings littered the ground.

The deed was done.

As Udin's hand receded, and the killing was complete, Mars fell to his knees, and he wept. The fury left him, and he was terribly cold. He shivered, bleeding steamy life onto the pine needles. On what shreds of Brann's kind face remained, his gaze was fixed. He owed him that. This sight he focused on until the black crept into his vision. The birds began to sing again, a breeze grew from the west, and he hung his mighty head like a Kathic statue. His blade fell from limp fingers, and his breathing stopped.

This was the moment the war of Duros-Tem began. This was the moment the light of the world dimmed.

Sages and acolytes in every corner of Alfheim felt a tremor. Portents of doom were scrivened and prophecies told. The time of peace was gone. Now, a shadow of death would come to the world: a black winged galleon of war. At its helm the Red Captain stood, and in hood's shadow he smiled.

10

It would begin as so many battles do: a cackling pack of robed madmen would run half naked through town.

Elisa, the odd, ironic guardian of Englemoor, brooded near the Ell River and considered a plan. She needed a way to draw out every pikeman, every constable, every guard in Englemoor. The lunatics would do nicely. In theory, this civil force she would then steer into the sewers, to battle back the horrors that multiplied there before their numbers grew too great.

To understand this plot, it is important to take note of the history of that area, for Englemoor was only the most recent occurrence of a settlement that dated back to an antediluvian past, when thick-browed beast men prowled the hills of the Greenway. Of that time very little remains, save a few standing stone dolmens at the edge of town, long since covered in ten feet of loamy grass.

But on the recent side of the great ice age, Englemoor was a place called Droon Rock. The karst topography of that area made it not only a flat, ideal town site, but its foundation stone was solid and easily hewn. Primitive men could both build and delve here, and so they did for centuries. Droon Rock was a timbered hall, farming village, and more notably, a labyrinth of burrows and tunnels that stretched all the way to the Rivers Ell, to the south and Furos in the west.

Not without a taint of shadow was this ancient place. In those tunnels blasphemous rites were chanted to long-forgotten gods. Great curving troughs were gouged to channel human blood from sacrificial pits, and piles of human bones had been found in the older caverns. What horrors those cave-dwellers and cloud-worshippers performed is mercifully lost to time, but the resonance of their shadowy purpose could not be washed away.

After the Age of Nurin, when the first true kings of mankind receded into memory, there was a long quiet on the central lands of Alfheim. Then was forgot Droon Rock entirely, and thick grass concealed old crimes red and whispered. In time, oblivious newcomers and their kin settled the area, lured by its bounty of usable quarries and river shores.

This folk were fur trading woodlings and fishermen. Ardenmoor they named their town, after their head family, and they clear cut the surrounding forests to build the roads and village sites that remain to this day. They were goodly, industrious folk, and brought the sun of reason to their time.

But the stain of eldritch wrong simmered beneath their foundations, and the town of Ardenmoor eventually fell on dark days. Plague and feud both wracked their happy respite. Murder became known to its people, and families cowered in their homes as reavers and avengers crisscrossed the moors like ghosts. Onto this decaying scene strode the Ardenwatch. These priestly knights bore new steel from the far south, and spoke with the silver tongues of saviors. In truth, however, they tortured their way into power, and hanged every dissenter in the name of order and law.

At its height, the Ardenwatch was a humming machine of punishment and ignominious death. Into cubic chambers below the town they packed their "suspects." Into these stone cubes would fifty or more innocent souls be stuffed and left to die. What a slow, horrible doom befell that poor folk in the lightless hell of the Arden cell-blocks. They starved, and resorted to cannibalism and far worse, only to die forgotten in heaps.

Like all tyranny, this one reached its zenith, and could not be endured. The Ardenwatch ended utterly in one horrible night of fire and frenzy. Townsfolk and their wild kin revolted with fury and cruelty on those false knights, and re-took their home with pike and torch.

Then, the long quiet of more modern times began. The name Arden was struck from every post and stone, and changed to Engle. Those that survived the horrors of the Ardenwatch were kinder, simpler folk, and held a firm grasp on reason with their humility. The town grew again, and in two centuries' time the night of Arden terrors faded into a story told by candlelight.

The tunnels lay abandoned. No soul dared those crypts and mass graves save the town watch, who used its uppermost catacombs to house the violent, the evil, and most of all the mad.

Who knows how such things gain momentum, but many settlements around the Greenway heard of the asylum in

Englemoor, where the insane could be held humanely, and ofttimes reformed to normalcy. To that town they wagoned their madmen, and with no dark purpose. The holding cells of Englemoor were sunlit in many cases, well cared for, and truly just. The insane were cared for in earnest, and with a gentle hand. It was a time of good and mercy, and pride was held for that place, though to many the mad can be unnerving.

So, the present day unfolded there. Arranged marriages made mighty the kin of neighboring lands, and Englemoor grew. It gained the problems of a larger city and shed its pastoral roots. The catacombs became a detail of little interest in the bustle of court life.

Always, though, the sensitive of that place could feel the shadow below the earth. Those musty halls were delved too far, and still harbored the echoing screams of a thousand ghosts. Deeds so terrible find a way of resurfacing in new forms, and denial is no tincture for the inevitable.

These housed lunatics would Elisa use to unify the town against the greatest threat it yet faced: that roiling, seething mass of tentacle things in the tunnels. If her last glance had told true, there were tens of thousands of them, each as strong as dwarven swordfighter and no easier to kill.

Elisa took a moment, washing in the morning steam, to consider her odd fate. What was this town or its people to her? Why had she chosen this fugitive vigilantism? Why not simply disappear into the Northlands and remain a hillwoman in peace?

The answer for her took not the same words as history tells, but held the same meaning. Hill folk of Alfheim, the children of great and mighty blood, harbor valor highest and ageless heroic instinct in their great hearts. They are the best of us, and never turn a cruel cheek to the trouble of others. They abide no shackle or injustice, like wild lions they are uncontainable, but righteous. Their kin are humble and blend into the woods like elk, but when doom threatens the weak they rise like a black anvil cloud.

So, the same responsibility rose in Elisa's heart. She would fight back this eldritch tide, take no credit, and be rid of Englemoor. Her conscience would be clear and she would return to the hills with bright eyes. Or perhaps she would wander east, toward Duros-Tem and the great stone doorways of the Dwarf Homes. Freedom was hers, and youth.

All she needed now was a few hundred swords to help in the fight. It would be a bloody day.

Elisa found her way to the Asylum tunnels, cramming her towering muscled form through a drain, 'round countless corners, and 'tween rusted out barricade bars. She was terribly strong, and the right purpose of the day made her more so. In those bright green eyes her blonde locks flitted with sweat and the morning damp, but she was set to a fight and a fight she'd find.

On her head, she donned the grim headsman's hood. She wasn't even sure why. Was it to conceal her acid burns, deny her accusers their wrath, or simply as a sort of battle ritual?

No matter. She donned it, and was a sight fit for the tunnels of Englemoor.

A few simple iron doors unhinged, a hatchway left open, and one addled guard knocked senseless and stowed in a broom closet was all it took. She crouched in a damp shadow and waited. In her mind's eye, she could see the enemy clear as day: writhing, multiplying things in the gloom. She would work to see that no lives were lost, but better ten guards now than a thousand innocents in a week's time.

The patients of Englemoor Asylum began to rub their eyes and creep out of their cells in disbelief. One, then three more, then a throng of them. The less restrained among them let loose a victorious cry, and all hell broke loose. They found the hatch, scampered to and fro like crazed rats, and hurled themselves into the sunlight, cackling with glee and comical exultation. Guards scurried, the warden cursed and raised a great bell tolling to the royal guard. Elisa's army was assembling.

The patients made a perfect mess of things. They were joyous, terrified, or simply arms outstretched, eyes closed, drinking in freedom like iced Gar. One robed inmate spotted The Headsman plainly, gave her a friendly nod, and went on his way, walking with an invisible cane to aid his regal stature.

The time had come. Plenty of guards, thugs, and sentries were in the streets above the Asylum. She caught the hatchway with a single hand, vaulted up like an ape, and stood wide-legged in the avenue just beyond the square. Her white linen raiments barely obscured her modesty, but beyond this, her impeccable musculature struck townsfolk, lunatic and guard alike, with awe and fear. The sunlight loved her form, and the very gods bowed their heads for her beauty.

"Over here, men of Englemoor!" she cried out above the din. "I'm the one you really want!" There was an awkward pause. All eyes met hers in the hood's eye slits, and she bellowed again, "Who will fell the Headsman?!"

At this taunt the warriors of that city could restrain themselves no more. They shoved their lesser charges aside, drew blades, banged shields, and set their toes toward her.

11

There are many peculiar things about dwarves that few know and even fewer believe. Some say their kin were hewn from solid rock in the ancient storm of the Primordius. Others believe they are proto-men whose line remained underground when the world was young.

In truth, they are human beings like all others, but stout and hearty as bears. Their famous traits were made through ages of hard lives in mines, high peaks, and snow-crusted plateaus north of Alfheim. There is no magic in their might, but for many they are easier to understand if it were so.

One undeniable truth of their folk is that they are very stalwart, and resistant to many of the frailties that haunt other folk. Even in death they cling to every drop of blood, every shallow breath. From cold sleep they can slowly revive, and even lay dormant for weeks as each slow heartbeat gains the strength to thump again.

It is this peculiar and noble quality that kept Mars from death's embrace in the forest clearing. In three days, his breathing resumed, and Hunnin awoke as well in his nearby glade. Neither had the strength to speak, and they crept like garden slugs across the dew to help each other. A small fire's warmth they shared, and another day spun overhead. No elf patrol came for them, no new doom appeared, but the gory ruin of the battle with Brann and the Red Captain were all too close. They had to rise, and regain their will, and move.

With no home to go to, and enemies teeming, their options were few and their resources even less. A run down old wagon found they, and a few scraps of pemmican. This they munched with sun-warmed wild cucumbers, but their bellies growled for Gar and Pork roast.

Hunnin, Hannar's father, was worse off than Mars. He had been smitten terribly on the head by that eldritch obelisk, and he wove in and out of consciousness like a fever. Mars helped him. Hunnin he placed in the wagon's wide bed, and took up the yoke himself. This sight few could dream would be: a captain of Fort Friendship bloodied and broken, pulling a wagon like a burro through the Greenway.

It is no longer known how long it took the hardy pair to reach the farm of Anna and Hannar. Was it two days, or two weeks? Not even Mars could recall, for he was beyond exhaustion. He knew of Hunnin's little house in the hills, and his strapping young son who dreamt of soldiering. Regardless, the farm was their only hope, for death was still very near for both dwarves.

It was late day when they reached the homestead. Bugs flitted in the low rays of amber. From the wooden door Hannar appeared. He was ruddy and healthy, but in his young eyes some fury burned. He appeared suddenly, and rigid, carrying a ragged wooden shield in one hand and an iron frying pan in the other. Mars had not the wits to wonder, and on seeing the boy collapsed. The wagon thumped to the grass.

Years later Mars would recall that Anna ran to them, and bound their wounds, and brought them in, but his memory of the weeks that passed since their arrival at the homestead consisted only of Hannar's stern face, and the cool safety of kitchen conversation.

"Up so early?" Anna asked Mars one morn. The wondrous smell of toasted oat Gar filled the front room.

"Aye, lass, and with half a wit to boot," Mars swung his legs from his nursing bed with a groan. He was finally awake again, and on the mend. His first thought went to Hunnin. "What of Hunnin?" he puzzled, rubbing his aching shoulder like a boxer.

"Sleeping, and still worrisome," Anna's voice trembled. She drew up a cup of the warm brown stout and brought it to Mars. Nothing is better to a dwarf than a metal mug of warm Gar for breakfast. His belly rumbled terribly. Anna saw the hunger in his face and did not make him ask.

"Don't worry," she added, turning back and toweling her hands, "bacon is crisping on the fire."

"You're a fine woman," Mars returned, "and Hunnin a lucky dwarf. Were we followed? Any sign of others?"

"Not since you arrived."

"And the boy?"

"Worried for his father, of course," she said. The biscuits were ready, and she brought them from the clay oven on a walnut board.

"Dark times are upon us, Anna my dear," Mars grumbled. He quaffed the warm Gar like a thirsty horse. "We must make haste to Ramthas. The King must be made to know."

Anna smiled. It took decades of strength to smile that smile. She was the wife of a warrior, the mother of an adventurer, and her patience was like a great oak in the Ravenwood.

"Time enough for wars and doom after breakfast," she said.

Mars laughed. It hurt his ribs like fire, but he laughed. With a nod, he finished his stout, then stood and walked to the window. It was a bright, hopeful morning. Songbirds made their cries, and the light was cool yellow floating through dandelion seeds and pine boughs.

Out in the yard, Hannar worked on the fence line. A fallen post he mended. The boy was his father's son, truly. For all his youth, he was built like a siege engine, with a neck as thick as his head and a nose as wide as the Greenway. His hands were soft, but broad as an axe and corded with knobby tendons and square knuckles. Mars was proud. He suddenly remembered poor Hunnin and broke his rest.

Anna recognized his sudden concern and nodded her head toward the next room. There Mars strode on bare feet. His refilled mug to be sipped (if a dwarf can ever sip a thing), he sat next to Hunnin's bed.

"Time enough for the black," he spoke in an oddly light tone, "time enough for snores, you old bear."

There was no response. Mars gulped the last of his Gar. It was foamed with beige perfection. The mug he set down, and reached out to Hunnin. On the shoulder he laid his hand, and that was when the horrors came.

From sleep Hunnin jerked awake at the touch. His eyes were wild and bulging like boiled eggs. A mighty hand rose he to Mars and slapped him brutally across the mouth.

"Away!" Hunnin cried. The yell broke the quiet of the farm terribly, and Hannar stopped to listen.

"Away from me, demon! Back to the abyss! Back to... back to the..." he faltered, shed a terrible tear, and slumped back into his bed.

Mars was wide-eyed and shocked. What had the Red Captain done to this hero? What nightmares still echoed in his battered brain?

Hannar burst into the house. "Pop!" he yelled, uncertain and excited. But the scene that greeted him was not what he hoped, and a feverish sweat beaded on his fallen father's brow. Mars looked up at Hannar with an apology, or comfort, he wasn't sure, and their eyes met.

"What happened?" Hannar asked, his tone entirely different. Blood oozed from Mars' lip. The room was grim.

"He's still a fever on him, my boy," Mars answered, wiping his split lip, "He's not himself."

Anna was shaken. She didn't know what to say, and walked over toward Hannar. She reached one hand out to him, but he pulled away. The sight of his pop laid low was beyond his young mind, and his view of the world and what would be was upended. Already fragile was the boy's heart, for he still remembered that awful day when they buried the two men near the woods. Men he'd throttled with his own hands.

Hunnin must have sensed the group in the room, for again he roused. His eyes cleared for a moment. Anna, Hannar and Mars all held their breath.

"Hannar, my son," Hunnin whispered. He smiled, and his mighty beard was bright.

Hannar did not respond. He was frozen. Those who have seen their parents at death's door know this terror.

"You've grown up strong, and with a fierce look, my boy," he went on, clearly straining, "On you falls the crest of our kin, Hannar lad. In you I place my trust."

This sounded like a goodbye. Hannar's eyes welled, his throat closed. He fought it back. Never would Hunnin see his tears. "Come closer, lad, let me see your muscles." He chuckled.

This broke Hannar's paralysis, and took one slow step. Slowly he reached up, and Hunnin took his forearm in the warrior's grip. His wide, knobby hand was strong as an ape.

"Hear me now, son. Burn these words in your courage." Hunnin inhaled, focused, exhaled.

"A true dwarf protects his kin, and abides no evil. A true dwarf stands as a great shield for the world. Like an anvil is he, and at times a storm cloud. So I was told, so were we all, back to the beginning." Hunnin paused, running out of strength. His son's eyes were locked on him, trembling.

"A true dwarf always drains his mug, loves his women, and stands like a brother to his friends. Dark will be your destiny, my boy. Few will be your words, but mighty will be your deeds. Lo, the kind hand of the New King will grace your brow, this I see in you."

Hannar could not hold his tears. The blood drained from Hunnin's great broad face. His grip weakened.

"Go. Go in my stead and learn from Mars. Care for your mother as she's cared for us, and let no shadow be cast on these good lands. I will see you at the great feast."

His voice faltered, his eyelids fluttered, and the wound on his brow from the eldritch stone flushed with dark red doom. There was a moment of perfect silence. The world seemed to fold in two. Then suddenly, Hunnin's breath returned, but in jerky gulps. His legs flapped like a fish, and he closed his claw-like grip around Hannar's arm with terrible fury. His neck went rigid, and his eyes rolled to their whites.

Mars knew this terror, and stood slowly. His hands sought something to defend them: a vegetable knife, a cleaver, an iron pot… anything. Anna was confused and scared, and Hannar opened his mouth in abject fear.

A violent gurgle escaped Hunnin's throat.

From his left shoulder there was a pop, then through the skin pierced a barbed whip of rubbery death. It was black and purple, ichorous with ooze. Hunnin, still aware in some remote way, grabbed the horror with his right hand, releasing Hannar.

From his sick bed he tumbled, but caught his feet, and stood wide-legged like a horseman. The things were within him, tearing and twisting, but he held. No mortal could do what that great dwarf did then, for he fought back the curse with sheer willpower, and regained his eyes. One last glance gave he to Anna, who loved him still.

He braced, compressing his chest and stomach into a rigid boulder of muscle. Another tentacle ripped out from a shin, splitting into four smaller squidlings. They sought Mars, and the boy Hannar, and even Hunnin's fair wife. They wanted more blood. It was time to take the only path.

Before Mars could raise his iron frying pot, Hunnin got one hand under his own jaw with effort. A foot slipped, and he caromed against the wall. Still he held. Still he held the snakes within him. That hand set, and prepared by raising his elbow. Then with one clean, mighty twist he snapped his neck like a pine bough.

The whips twitched and died, and little blood flowed. In the rays of a window did Hunnin find his rest at last, and he had made safe his family with a final act of true courage. His blood had held true. The gods would be pleased, and he could walk among his noble kin with no shame in the halls of forever.

For those left behind, the scene was grim, and impossible. But there that warm yellow ray fell through paned color, and Hunnin's beard glowed like a star.

So ended the great captain of Fort Friendship. So Mars became its final survivor. So the terrible wrath that would consume Hannar the Shieldmaster was forged.

12

A dwarven funeral is no small thing. Grief runs like a river through every heart, but its pain is compounded by a resonating joy. All those moments made rich by heroic hearts, all those deeds done by weathered hands, all those cries lifted up for the gods to hear... They make a wondrous din of things.

At the base of a boulder was Hunnin laid to sleep, in a square cairn his ashes set. So was the way of the hill folk of that time north of the Greenway. The three of them composed a tiny and lonely funeral party.

Anna was beautiful in the spring light. Her blonde braids cascaded past ribbon bow epaulets. Tied with green thread were her silken sleeves. Those great wide eyes of hers set on a face of softness and barely parted lips. Her strength never more evident in detail and posture, no queen was more noble as she filled three great wooden mugs with Hunnin's favorite Golden Gar.

As for Mars, he too held a sunlit demeanor. He leaned on the great boulder like a loitering bard, and told tales all afternoon. Hunnin's great stand against the blue orcs of Thod, the time Hunnin navigated a fleet of warships through a soupy fog at Dagger Bay, or the time they went sledding on their shields after the battle of Ramthas. Two kings had they seen as friends, and more centuries. Mars banged his steel gauntlets on that mossy boulder, and spoke of the dwarven homes beyond the stars where great hewn blocks of the noblest granite housed the heroes of yore, where Hunnin would learn all the wonders of time itself, and look down on the mortal world with a beard of lightning.

Great braided ropes were tied from every tree to the gable post at the front stoop. White butterflies filled the air, and Anna strummed her lute as best she could, playing "Forge of Ice, Forge of Fire," "The Battle of Hammers" and "Fool's Mug" all Hunnin's favorites.

One face remained dour. One face peered up from mug's edge with fury: Hannar's. Even though young, he was well of age to taste Gar, and not new to it. He quaffed from his towering mug, and rivulets ran down his chin. He was a foot shorter than Mars with youth, but his eyes seemed ancient and gloomy as a dragon's. On that small pile of stones his gaze was fixed, and no song could stir him. He heard nothing, only a roaring hum of rage between his ears. Too soon had he learned of death.

Night was closing in, and the mugs took their toll. Mars would not leave the cairn, but rested there beside it, chatting with his old friend casually. At length, he turned to brooding Hannar.

"Brighten your face, my boy! We dwarves face not death with frowns and fear."

"I'm not afraid." Hannar murmured, not looking up.

"Then grief stricken, fair enough," Mars replied, ready to test the boy's choler. "You do your father proud by lifting that chin, and showing the bright heart of our folk. His was a life of heroism, not just a death in darkness."

"What heroism is there in sitting here like winter toads while those who did this walk unavenged?" Hannar took one last look at his mug, emptied it with a gulp, and threw it into the woods. His nostrils flared and he ground his teeth like a tiger.

"Mind your wits, son," Mars counseled gently. "We'll do no revenging tonight. Our first task is to the New King, the heir called Akram who has taken up the throne in Ramthas. He must know of this treachery."

"A messenger's errand," Hunnin's son spat back, clearly targeting Mars. This was an unwise tactic, but he was hot with youthful wrath, and beyond reason. His mind was already made up. He just needed the opportune moment.

Mars stood with this comment. In any other moment, such insolence would have earned a dwarven boy a split lip. But Mars stayed his anger, for he knew the boy was baiting him.

"I'll forgive your tone for Hunnin's honor, son. You'll do as right demands and the three of us will make journey to Ramthas at dawn. Your mother is already-"

"As RIGHT demands?"

"Aye. We've duty to King and Crown before personal vendetta and you know it. You've much to learn besides how to bash with a shield." There was a too-long pause.

"Perhaps you are afraid," Hannar muttered under his breath. Before the words escaped his lips he regretted saying them, but young folk often do such things. Mars took a long slow breath, gently set his mug at Hunnin's grave-side, spilling not one drop, and took a step toward his friend's son.

"I'm not sure I heard you, Hannar," he said to the youngster. Hunnin would approve of this lesson and he knew it. "Care to repeat that last bit?"

Hannar could not look up at him. He was fuming, but even at that moment knew he was in the wrong. He thought long as Mars stared him down. "I said... Maybe you're right."

In a way, Mars was more disappointed with this answer than the insult. He huffed through his nose and returned to his mug, rolling one shoulder to break the tension in his neck.

At that boulder of grief Anna stayed the night, wrapped in a checkered blanket. Mars dozed off in the patio rocking chair, and the frost of evening crept up. When the sparrows started singing, Anna shook off the chill and rose first.

Immediately she knew something was wrong. The house was quiet, Mars grumbling in his sleep like a bear. Hannar was nowhere to be seen. She went inside, and when she saw that his wooden shield was not in its usual spot by the kitchen bread bin, she knew for certain.

Her son had gone.

13

At the head of the Black Mountains, east of the widest part of the Greenway, but far above the plains that slope to the great wall of Duros-Tem, there stands a knife of rock and piney crags that splits the mists like the mast of a warship. This rock is called Ramthas, named for the hillman king who cut its foundations into a fortress of solid basalt.

That dynasty was lost when elves took the city five centuries ago. Under their kind and glowing rule Ramthas was expanded upward, and festooned with narrow pinnacles. When darkness crept into their immortal hearts, their rule faltered, and Ramthas was returned to the hands of men and dwarves.

This is but one of many barbs that gave the wars their sting in those times.

It is important to note the generations that rose and fell on that high seat of royalty, for when the young King Akram strode out to greet his old friend Mars, the tones of history were thick in the banners.

Before Akram came three great kings in one line; there was the man called Ethred, his son Uthred, and his dwarven heir Akkred. The third of these is perhaps the most interesting, for with dwarven wife did Uthred share his royal bed. She was a noble and beloved queen named Keel. Her folk were none other than the door-cutters of Tem, the deep delving dwarves that held the world's backbone safe from all the horrors that lurk below the foundations of Alfheim. Their union made mighty the good people of that time, but laid low the deposed elves.

So it was that Akram, only a dozen years hence, had inherited the crown from the son of Uthred, King Akkred. His ties to the Temmish were solid as stone, his blood a blend of all the best of men, and his rule just with the aid and council of aged scholars.

But deposed was not a state beloved by the once-noble elves, and ever did they pine in shadow for restoration, or even vengeance. This aching wound found its root in the treachery of the spider Lydea, and in the hideous hate of Red Fang, whose name would soon come to symbolize the black vexation of the forbidden underworld.

Akram, though, strode above all this. Even in his bright-eyed youth he made a good king. Barely a century under his boots had he, but his judgements were measured and his hand firm. And yet, Akram knew of war only what he had learned as a plated archer and hammerman in the campaigns of Helm and the frontiers of Kath. A score of battles only had he endured, so when Mars approached with his brow in a knot, uncertainty hung in the air like salt.

This was the context of Akram's first great war, and somehow he knew this. Ruin, that gleaming and horrible weapon of Mars', caught his mind's eye in the knowing. In the reflection of that endless blade saw he all that would come next: shadow, and wrath, and deeds crimson with inevitable savagery.

"Mars!" Akram bellowed, seeing the warrior of Fort Friendship in the open-air court, "A hero's boots grace the rock of Ramthas! Mugs!" A cheer arose, but Mars did not raise a fist, or laugh, and the mugs were brought in a quiet.

Mars walked up to the great and bright-eyed king, and took a knee. Behind him was Anna, Hunnin's wife. She smiled and bowed low.

"Rise, you old badger," Akram prodded. He tugged the dwarf up by one arm, and was surprised by the weight of the warrior. He was like a boulder.

"Pardon my mess and blade, my King," Mars apologized, looking the Falcon right in the eye, "but I bring ill news, and an urgent errand."

"News is never ill, my friend, only the grim work that follows. Lift your heart for now, as I've not seen a dwarf as fierce as you in a year! Gods, you've become grizzled as iron!" This lifted Mars' heart, and for a moment he forgot the horror in the woods of Ell, and the rocky cairn of Hunnin his best friend.

The three of them, Akram's queen Ezra, and the elite guard all sat to take a mug. The elite were men and women alike, of many shapes, and they bore a sunlit air. Their armor was polished and bright, and each carried the blocky hammer of Akram's sigil in an iron belt loop.

The Gar in the royal larder was the finest Mars had ever known. It was golden and clear, but rich and crisp with the plump hops of the shipbuilders of Port Frost. He emptied his octagonal mug in two great quaffs, smiled at Anna, and began.

"My King, the elves have broken the treaty. Fort Friendship is no more, and this is the least of our woes. Some new darkness has come into being, with a Red Captain at its fore."

The wide-brimmed braziers of the chamber burned low into the night. A slow breeze wandered through the granite windows and angular arches of Akram's hall. A sympathetic arm 'round Anna's lovely shoulders had the king, and he heard the tale. Mugs littered the broad oak table.

"What of Hannar?" Akram asked at last. Anna's eyes lowered.

"We've no idea," she answered, "He took to the woods with a wrathful heart. He moves like an elk through the dells, so we knew we must come here first. But he is my son, and tough as leather. I've all faith in Udin he will not only survive out there, but seek out this Red Captain..."

Akram squeezed her shoulder with a gentle love. "Then we share your son's purpose, and with a brigade of my finest. Word will be sent to Uthiel, Queen of Kath. If war she wants, then she'll have it. If these traitors be rogue, then she'll send a flight of archers to aid us in rooting them out."

Mars bowed his head. It was a wonder to behold a decisive king.

"But first, we sleep! No deed should be undertaken by candlelight in a mess of mugs!" He smiled a wide, true smile.

Here his kingship found its root, for that smile brightened every heart at the table.

"I am not done yet my King!" said one of the elite, rising from his bench, a sloshing, brimming mug in his blocky fist. "This golden Gar I drink for Hunnin! At Dagger Coast he was my captain, and a great one! We go in his name, and all the brave of Fort Friendship! With bright hearts!" The mug he splashed onto his beard and guzzled in an instant. Such a feat few could muster, especially late in the evening, and a cheer arose.

That night they all slept well, save grumpy old Mars. He leaned on an oaken column in the firelight, and slowly sharpened the endless edge of Ruin with a grim look.

"You'll be avenged yet, my brother." The orange light danced across the tremendous blade in rivulets of reflection. The groove was clean and silver as the moon, etched in bluish runes and filigree. The antler guard braced on one thigh, he edged it to a deadly perfection. A razor made for one gut, sharp enough to hack that hideous obelisk in two if need be. Its shape drifted and taunted him behind his eyes as he finally fell asleep, only to dream of his Brann's death in that lonely glen. Only to dream of those rubbery black whips unmaking all the right of the world. Only to dream of the Red Captain's eyes as he was run through by the inevitable wrath of Ruin.

14

Having annihilated the soldiers at Fort Friendship, the Red Captain had only begun his campaign of terror. The elves of his time had proven impotent and cowardly. Silently they watched as the impudent races spread and multiplied like rats on their lands.

There was a time when he was like them: paralyzed with inaction. There was a time when he was mortal. That time had passed, for unto him was delivered the harbinger of a future undreamed of: The Devourer. At least, that is what he called it.

It was not a creature, or even a being. It was a sort of place or phenomenon. At the coiling fulcrum of time and space it twisted and twitched with meaningless music. On black lakes of infinite hells it slid and slurped through the eons in the nightmares of men, and spun impossibly at the center of all things. It was the eater and the scream, the poison rain and the choking toad. It was the eel behind his eye and the howling silence of cold starless space.

And it was his master.

Fortunate are the weaklings of the world, ignorant and irrelevant in the womb of futility. They know nothing of the frigid faces of the true gods, who live above and outside the black dimensions that govern our titanic universe with cold, inevitable hunger. The Red Captain was no such mewling, and dared the pits below Xanos to reveal their terrors.

Only with spell and shield did he survive that abode of evil, and he returned from his pilgrimage immortal and touched by the slithering whips of The Devourer. He returned bent on the uprooting of the world. A dead world would make a fitting welcome for the god-thing in folding triangles of insanity, and he would make it so.

This was the least you need know of the Red Captain to understand what came next; he made way to the Plain of Kellan.

Two weeks' march was it for most from the Greenway, but the winds of hate pushed him and his dead squadron forward with a stallion's haste. They did not run, or ride skeletal mares, but moved in a sort of coiling smoke. They left little track and less sound.

Within a few nights they topped Fist Rock, and looked down on the forbidden lands. The plain sloped upward to the impossible sheer face of Duros-Tem, the Iron Wall, and ghosts moaned on the wind.

Of this journey, only one mortal soul had knowledge. Only one wild-eyed hunter had the foolish courage to pursue such a force. Only one avenger was so hungry with wrath and blind fury to dash through the trees like a tiger hunting its prey: Hannar, Hunnin's son.

15

It began as many quests do: a disheveled schoolboy stumbled into a fruit cart, spilling a mess of melons and gourds in a clatter. At the head of a column of gleaming pikemen strode King Akram of Ramthas, and the boy was beside himself, grinning like a camel.

The good King chuckled, helped the star-shocked boy to his feet, and received a cheer from the city yard. Ramthas was built in a series of stone chevrons that flanked the great rock formation at the main tower's head. It was blocky, irregular, and nestled in the foothills like a gulch. High thin banners drifted from oak poles thirty feet long, while silver etchings bewildered the eye on every tower door and gate-bench.

From the main front gate strode the King, and took pause. Words were not counted among his many strengths, but inevitable at this moment. He turned back toward the balustrades of the fortress, and met the gaze of two thousand citizens.

"Good people," he began in his normal kingly tone. But his momentum broke, and he was distracted. High on that craggy breeze was caught a great bird of prey. It was fast, and smaller than an eagle. It darted and soared in weaving wonders of flight. A shrill cry broke the moment.

The King smiled at the sight of this.

"Heroic family of Ramthas, Rock of Ages, Kathic freedom fighters! Hear me!" The crowd cheered like wild. Only a warrior king could know to call those careful words, to say so little of tradition and make it matter.

"We go to answer the murderous elves of Fort Friendship," he began with a grim change, "and justice will be done." There was a long pause, and all fell silent.

"For all the years my Father cared for this wondrous place, no war broke 'tween elvenkind and the men and dwarves of Duros. So noble a deed I'll not know, it seems!" He let himself think, and smiled at the boy, who stood tall.

"But if war is what they crave, they'll find not vengeance, or rage, or an eager sword, but the keen, patient, wise and righteous *shield* of the people of Ramthas Rock!" Boots were banged on cheese boards, spoons on pans, and great mountain voices raised in answer.

"We go to find out what happened, and we'll send word the moment we know. Until then, remain vigilant. The mountains have made you strong! Show me!"

At this they went solemn, and united in a deep roar. A hundred or more young warriors stood forward, and took the knee with helm under arm. Akram's name they grunted in unison. The old ways held fast.

Akram paused the march with a raised fist. The crowd hushed. He walked, frowning and dour, over to the warrior troupe. They were stone still. One by one he examined them. His brow was a knot, and his disapproving beard flared forward like a horse's tail.

Then finally, he stopped in the center of them. From side to side glanced he, and let fly a battle cry. It was a simple, short barking yell, like a bear falling from a tree. All the soldiers jumped to their feet, slammed inward in a heap, and embraced their King. He hugged every one of them, and laughed, and they lifted him up and over like a barrel of Gar.

Even Anna, dark with worry, smiled at that moment, and knew this King would lead them to her son, and she would be at his side.

Again, the King, laughing, gave a great bark. The soldiers went rigid again, to one knee, and the gates opened. From Ramthas marched they and headed southwest to Fort Friendship... or whatever smoldering doom remained of it.

Four days' march went swiftly by and the decimated fort was in view. The scene was grim, crows circled low above the ramparts, and a gloom hung above the bodies like an impatient reaper. The scene was untouched from a fortnight before save by the vermin and birds. They had picked at the noble souls and had their share, but the enemy left no dead. Mars shuddered.

Slowly, solemnly, they picked through the rubble. King and soldier alike did the dark work of burial. Helms were hung, boots tied, eyes gently closed. A full complement of dwarves and men lay slain there, more than fifty in all.

Mars could feel his blood heating. The King sensed this and comforted him with a broad hand. No words broke the quiet.

At length, one of Akram's elite strode forth, and the burials were complete. He was called Hauser, a woodsman by trade and master tracker.

"My King," he began. The words cracked through the funeral silence like an ice bath. Akram nodded and bade him go on. "A track, arriving from the southwest, and departing out at the northeast corner, but with a group of dwarves in the fray."

"Our company, as I told you," Mars muttered. "We made our stand half-day's walk that way, at the edge of the Nellman Groves."

"We tend those fallen first," Akram announced without hesitation. His rage was seething, but his bright brow and green eyes cooled the scowl.

Hauser rose and mobilized the Elite. They were a brigade of fifteen scale-clad warriors, each with bow, quiver, and longhammer. They followed the track out toward the Groves, and Mars drug his boots. He did not want to return to that place.

He got his wish.

Not half the distance to the resting place of Wrimm, and Scratch, and Brann, Hauser raised his fist and crouched. Movement ahead. The column halted. Akram squinted in the afternoon glare.

Ahead, at the edge of the woods, something very large writhed and waved among the tree trunks. It was hard to make out, but with patience the company caught a clear look at last. Like a giant hydra or great wavering tangle of cobras, a cluster of snake-like shapes danced among the trees. They coiled and whipped and wrapped 'round the oaks with wet slapping sounds. One curled and twitched a moment in the clear, its underside was visibly adorned with rows upon rows of tiny hooked barbs.

"Gods," Akram hissed.

"It grows with each day my King," Mars whispered, lowering his head a bit. "They were but eels and whips when we fought. Udin's Hand, they're huge."

"Hauser, Kray, Whitefeather. You three double back. We follow the track of the attackers." The King was stern and no longer soft. This was a peril beyond the normal world. "Mind your backs, lads."

The three warriors nodded and made off quietly. The rest followed. The track was faint, barely readable, and led to a bluff two days beyond. From there the group could survey the town of Englemoor in the distance. The track vanished.

"No sign beyond here," Hauser reported.

"Why lay waste to a garrison, then simply make off for parts unknown?" Anna asked. She scanned the horizon with a mother's worry. "What is brewing here, my Lords?"

"Not war," Mars retorted with a huff, "this is sorcery."

Akram said nothing. His whiskers stood on end. Then he flinched, and leaned forward on one knee, squinting into the distance. "What in blazes..." He pointed. His knotted arm was thick as a tree trunk, and clad in segmented brass plates. Each plate was hinged into the next, and chisel-etched with the chevron inlay of Ramthas Rock. It was a sight to behold, and commanded the attention of the entire company.

They all turned, and strained their eyes, for Englemoor was still barely a lump on the far horizon of hill and hedgerow. From that spot rose one thin column of dark smoke. As they brought it to focus, something moved, and one of the taller buildings crumbled before their eyes.

It was the high hall of Grimwald. That tower was a four-story masterpiece of the Ardenmoor days: stone and pine all spiraling upward to high thin parapets and a ring of thin red banners. Now it crumbled, slumping into a heap and vanishing in the remote roofline without sound.

"Hauser, up front. Kray at the tail. Make haste, warriors!" Akram was barely finished with this order before hopping down from his rocky perch, assisting Anna, who needed no help, and bounding forward. Mars slung Ruin on his shoulder like a lodge pole and joined the run.

In less than an hour they were at Englemoor's outer wall. The sun was low now, and long amber shadows yawned through the billowing smoke that arose from days-old fires. The town was in complete ruin... A husk. The outer wall was crumbled to tatters in a dozen places, but no military occupied or marched or barked. There was an ominous, low quiet that hung in the scorched air. The wind was rotten and musty.

For one brief moment, the breeze rose, and the smoke slid away. Anna caught a glimpse of the opening causeway of the town, which was a wide cobbled pave. There were no bodies, no movement, and every other building had its walls exploded out or smashed inward. It made no sense, and reason could not confine it.

"No sound," Akram gestured, mouthing the words. He lay an open hand slowly downward, the gesture for stealth and wary eyes. When he moved, they all moved, and no other time. Only the occasional jangle of armor betrayed their steps as they entered the ruin of Englemoor.

16

It ended as so many great chases do: a little boy was breathing fire.

His lungs were like the dwarven forges of yore, a bellows heating his veins. His thighs were molten rubber on wobbly rattan knees. One boot was flapping apart like a sandwich thrown into the street, and every knuckle was bloodied and raw. Hannar, Hunnin's son, gave chase. He was like a feral predator smelling blood. His hunger was beyond mere sustenance; he hungered for vengeance, and was too young to understand its dark effect on those who lose themselves in its throes.

Thoughtless, he pressed forward. He had caught a faint track from Fort Friendship heading east. Every so often the track vanished entirely, and he had to go on instinct, or trace the subtle scent of elven steel. The process they used to burnish and harden their breastplates left a coppery aroma on the metal, and in numbers that smell could be caught by a dwarf of the old blood. Hannar was this and more. He had left all he ever cared for on this quest, and did not intend to fail.

Tracked they he over hill and dale beyond the Greenway's rolling slopes. Through that bouldered alluvial plain called Nuras' Nest, and ever eastward to the foothills of Urin Pinnacle. There they had camped, but made no fire and cooked no meal. He gained on them. They slowed at last on the Plain of Kellan, at Fist Rock. Much later this place would be called Siege Rock, and the Plain of Bones. But that great war had not yet come. For now, the scene was plenty to behold.

Fist rock spiked outward from the pinnacles at an impossible angle. Its defiant point leaned one hundred feet above the valley floor, and came to a table-like point. Beyond its wondrous mass, due east, stood the greatest monument of the known world: The Wall of Duros.

Hannar fell to his battered knees on that rocky edifice as tears streamed down his mud-smeared cheeks. All his anger broke for a moment. The beauty of this great work was beyond any story he had heard, or what any tall tale could boast.

The thing stretched into the curving, fogged distance in both directions. Above the plain it towered like a mountain range. Its blocky towers dared the lowest drifting clouds, and were capped with snow at those impossible heights. So colossal was this cyclopean titan, it dizzied the mind to feel its weight exploding straight up from the plains below. Tiny windows, doors, and stairways dotted the surface like goat trails on a peak, and wide-winged eagles soared in circles on its drafts and breezes.

But on this wonder no banner flew. No color defied the endless expanse of hewn stone. No wooden gable post or banded door broke the ageless granite infinity. The air was silent and forever between Fist Rock and the wall's mind-bending scale. It was a place the mortal mind could perceive the profound scale of the universe, and feel the turning, folding, ageless breathing of the cosmos itself.

So, he cried.

He cried for his father. He cried for his mother in her timeless stoic smile. He cried for the dead men he killed with his bare hands. He cried for the corpses at Fort Friendship. Most of all, he cried for himself. At this his anger returned, for the last emotion felt like weakness, and the old blood wouldn't have it.

Stood he then, tall as a tree on Fist Rock's promenade. His blonde fop drifted in a gust of wind, and his shield was motionless on his right hand. Through his broad dwarven nostrils he took that clean, massive air. This monument was the work of *his* folk. This feat of endurance, of patience, of unity-a reminder of all that could be when folk join in purpose-was *his*. Not lightly would this duty pass from those countless unseen generations of yore into his veins. Not lightly would the honor of his folk rest on his shoulders, so he crouched, his eyes narrowed again, and scoured he that wide plain for any sign of his prey.   A wiry plume of black smoke betrayed the vastness of the plain. It spiraled and coiled upward, made tiny by the massive grey backdrop of the wall. It was a garrison at the wall's foot, part in flames. The distance was too far to see more. No doubt it was the next stop on his quarry's path of destruction.

What could their purpose be? What drove them across the landscape with such fury and speed? Hannar didn't even know who or what they were save Mars' report that they were an undisciplined rabble of elven traitors. After this chase, Hannar could not have known, but they were something far more sinister.

In leaps and sliding strides, he found his way down onto the grassland and through the dells that formed that wide valley floor. By dusk he was at the destroyed garrison. Again, he was aged beyond his years at that moment. Bodies. Dwarves and men all tangled and twisted in steel and blood.

Hardened this time, Hannar did not pause. He scoured for track, and found their way forward. The elves had been forced to take to the wallways, as the bedrock of this mighty edifice was too dense to cut any dungeon or passage. The only way was over.

To understand what happened next, it is important to know how the Dwarves of Duros managed such a feat of engineering. The Wall was in fact not built, but hewn. Over generations were the roots of the mountain cut back, and a series of cranes and counterweights hoisted the boulders and till above. Here was stacked and fitted a mighty retaining wall, which was in turn backfilled by smaller skree and rubble from the base.

Over four hundred years this process continued, cutting inward, hoisting and stacking, along forty leagues of solid stone. The upper half was riddled with cavities, chambers, tunnels and gateways, but the root of the wall was a mind-bending single mass of solid rock. The first precarious doorway did not defy the sheer face of it until at least two hundred feet straight up.

These doorways and signal fire stations were accessed by zig zagging stairways, death-defying hand hold ladders, and foot-stone traversals that gave the wall a brocade appearance from miles off. Up these dizzying paths the elves had gone, and Hannar began to follow.

But in moments, something felt off. There were no iron boot marks on these steps. The elves had passed here, that was certain, but no dwarf had taken this path. In fact, some of the handholds had crumbed away, and the next were beyond dwarven reach. Hannar stopped, surveyed the dizzy scene, and saw his answer clear as day.

What he passed by as a service or trash tunnel had new relevance. He returned five strides downward, no easy task at these heights, and looked inside the square opening. It was shallow, and blocky-cut. The rear wall was only a few feet inward, and then a connecting shaft shot straight upward into darkness. One wall was cut with a slotted groove that held a small rectangular step. The opposite wall was grooved as well, but empty. Hannar recognized this dwarven invention.

On the shelf he stood, and his weight gave a click behind the stone. From above, a grinding, and the tiny stoop slid upward. He braced and rode the stone at speed. Halfway up the counterstone slid downward past him, and light glowed above.

This manner brought him to a wall-top station in moments, while the elves must have taken hours to make the climb. Hannar popped his knuckles on Wall's leather grip, and he smelled a fight ahead.

Now, elves are not known to handle disappointment well, or abide being humbled by the other races of Alfheim. Their pride and lofty self-worth is age-old, and ingrained in their bloodlines like letters etched in marble. So it was that pang of surprise and foolish hubris was known to them that day, and stung it did.

At the pinnacle of Duros' mighty wall stood a lone dwarf, barely twelve winters in his boots, disheveled shield in one hand and weaponless, grinning ear to ear like some foolish devil about to breathe hellfire.

The Red Captain stopped suddenly, having just crested the final stairway. He was winded, and the entire company needed rest despite their unnatural bloodless life force. Before them the dwarven boy stood defiant in the high, cold wind. Snow gathered at the granite corner jambs, and flurries drifted about the boy's golden braids.

In his left hand, he held a rusted steel pole bannered with the great thin linen of Duros' folk: a dark red taper with a single black chevron at the center. The high winds caught this ancient cloth, and it flew and whipped above the youth like a scene from the sagas.

It was a good day to fight.

"I am Hannar, Hunnin's son," he began, "and this is Wall." He lifted the shield in front of him, banging on it with the banner pole. "Come take it from me, *if* you can."

The Red Captain was wide-eyed, gasping, and frigidly pale in that snowy air. This was the ground of dwarves, and no place for elvenkind. Their skin was too thin, their blood to close to the cold, their ears nipped with ice.

Despite all this, he laughed.

"Fool! What know you of our purpose? Of anything?" He straightened his crimson cloak dismissively, and waved his right hand with a lazy gesture. His company of elves, fifty strong at least, covered in scrapes and dented armor and battle wear, exploded forward.

The battle was joined. The tale of that day has been told more than even the campaigns of Kellan the Conqueror, or the exploits of the dragon slayers of the First Age. Rightly so, for that day a young boy met the supernatural onslaught of evil head on, and did not flinch.

17

It's a curious thing how time can slow during the moments of greatest intensity in life. The mind digs its heels in, refuses to let the moment slip by, and magnifies time through the lens of white hot attention. It raises the question of what relationship truly exists between time and perception.

Now the scribners of old Ardenmoor, zealots in scholars' robes and little else, posited that time heeded only the will of the One God...that the passing of each moment was evidence of His heartbeat, and the pace of this was not only fixed but a cosmic law. So, men toiled and triumphed in the shadow of a temporal universe so far beyond themselves it practically gloated with titanic distance.

Opposing this frigid view were the desert priests and hermits of Koab, that strange domed city at the edge of the Ghost Sands. To them, time was a construct of the mortal mind, present only to aid in our instinct to make sense of a formless, pulsating, cyclical dimension called now.

Few of these book-makers and vision-havers had much evidence either way, for they had not known the odd nature of time in the heat of battle. Whitefeather, the tallest, swiftest, and quietest of Akram's elite soldier brigade, knew of this. He knew of this with acute clarity in the last seconds of his life.

Whitefeather's knuckles turned stark white, and he lost his grip for a split second. The leather-wrapped haft of the longhammer creaked and frayed. There was no way out. Below, a yawning pit crackled and crumbled. It was more like a fissure or chasm in the heart of Englemoor. Above this dangled he from the hammer's grip. The pit teemed and tangled with blackish rubbery things. They were like a giant squid, but eel-like in shape individually, and their mass sickened the mind with the darkness of that hideous plane from which they must have ebbed.

At the hammer's other end was a form of legend. It was The Headsman. She was three hands taller than Whitefeather, broad as a beer wagon at the shoulders, and strung with crushing thews like steel cables. Her muscled form was covered with remnants of armor, cloth scraps, and frog belts in various tangles. A half-dozen weapons were lashed and looped at her waist, and she sported only one boot.

With one mighty fist she held the hammer fast, saving Whitefeather's life for a brief second. With the other she held a snaking purple whip at bay. Its barbed suckers smacked and strained to reach her throat. Her chest stretched impossibly between the two efforts, and her hood was peeled back enough to show white, bare teeth in a silent hellscream of sheer will.

Facing this choice, atop the sagging roof of the Wrong Way Tavern, she again found that unexpected valor of her folk. In one action, she let the tentacle snap 'round her neck like a cobra. It burned, she choked, and brought the other hand to the hammer. Like a great mythic athlete of Aphos, she swung the hammer, soldier in tow, to one side. Whitefeather took her cue and released at the zenith of the swing, tumbling through mid-air toward solid ground.

But it was for naught. As he wheeled through the air with a final hope, one massive arm of slime-oiled death snapped out from the pit below, coiled around him with a crushing wet slap, and yanked him brutally into the black. Only the wrenching squeals of crushing armor accompanied his doom.

"Damnit!" Elisa spat. The eel at her neck she tore away and crushed, then surveyed the scene. The fight had not gone well. Not well at all.

The guard of Englemoor had fought bravely enough in the first few days, and when the maniacs of the asylum catacombs took up arms and turned their wild howls toward the enemy, the tide had briefly turned. But these abominations spewed from some unseen depth below the city, and only multiplied when defeated.

Elisa and a company of the living had backed themselves into Seras' Cathedral at the south edge of town. The stone walls and foundation proved impermeable to the tentacle-things, who picked the city clean by night and mostly absconded to the tunnels by day.

But the light of Seras could be their shield for only so long. They had no provisions, and a half-dozen of Elisa's improvised militia were bleeding out. So, they made for the Wrong Way Tavern, stealthy as shadows.

That was three days past, and in perfect silence they had eluded the creatures for that time... But to what end? Elisa constantly questioned why they were fighting the endless enemy; Why not skulk out of the city by day?

Some foolish honor pecked at her, though, and at her companions. Half mad with blood and days of fighting, watching townsfolk torn apart, buildings swallowed, or bleary-eyed madness taking the weak-willed into the pit on their own feet, the survivors of Englemoor were weary indeed. Still they had to resist these fell things. They had to.

So, when Akram's company came slinking into town that afternoon amid the smoke and ruin, Elisa's stealth was betrayed, and the things sniffed them out again. They erupted from the earth like a wave in a fumarole, shattering pine and tile alike. Akram's company braced and gasped, having no idea what in the hells was happening.

Elisa had saved them, rallied them, and returned to her safe haven at the Wrong Way, but for naught. The eels of death filled every cavity, and had mutilated half the King's elite before any good fighting ground could be gained.

That is when Whitefeather, a heroic, slender youth of Kathic blood but raised in Ramthas' shadow, was lashed by the whips and pulled to his grave. The tavern was crumbling, and Anna and Mars fought the creatures back at the cellar rubble while Akram, Elisa and the others made a stand at the shattered opening that was once the second floor.

"We must be rid of this place!" Akram bellowed, smashing a purple tangle with an iron boot. "We'll not last another minute!"

"Headsman!" a robe-clad militiaman called. He was in random pieces of armor and slung with swords on both hips. "Look!" He pointed straight down.

Elisa looked as the gaping pit below them was suddenly emptied. The seething beasts withdrew from that fissure impossibly fast, and two more chasms cracked open at either side of the building.

"It means to crush us!" Anna cried out, taking refuge behind Mars, and bumping into the tangle of elite soldiers and ragtag lunatics.

Elisa's gaze met Akram's. It was an odd moment, for she was four heads taller than he at least. They both had that shine in their eyes, though: the gleam of the mighty. There was silent understanding in that split second. Both heroes breathed in, nodded their heads inexplicably at each other, and braced on the crumbling gable. The only escape lay straight down.

"If we mean to fight," Akram laughed, hands on hips, "then let's pierce the thing in the heart!" He waved the others to follow, looped his hammer at his waist, for the legendary Angrid had not yet been found, and leapt like a frog into mid-air. Down into the opening he flapped and vanished in the dim.

"Back into the bloody tunnels, lads!" Elisa yelled, and every hope of a quick victory, every intent of walking away from this accursed town and returning to the hills faded. She leapt, and they all followed. Anna went last, hacking a purplish worm-grabber from her boot with a hatchet at the last moment.

Just as the company vanished, the things gathered their force on both sides of the building, and clasped together in a slimy crash of splinters and shattered stone. The entire structure exploded into dust, and the barb-lined suckers probed at the ruin for signs of prey, but they had gone.

So, Englemoor fell silent again, and those cobbled paves were not trod by mortal men for three generations after that day.

18

Alfheim had not always been a den of formless monsters and evil wizards. In fact, the more it became a wild and unbelievable place, the less its stories meant for generations to come. There is much in the small and commonplace that the wondrous and epic can never capture. Alas, the wondrous came to Alfheim, but as watchers of those ages from the distance of time, we must remember to seek out the minute and mundane things to truly know what our predecessors sacrificed for us.

In its earliest days, fresh from the baffling crucible of the Primordius, this land was a great sprawling wilderness teeming with bears, wolves, mice and birds. There were no men, or dwarves, or sorcerers or treacherous elves. There were no great works of architecture, or strange vine-choked temples in the damp.

But like all things, the world was changed by time. The nobler gods, great towering avatars of truth and forever, were envied and despised by the lesser. Behind all this the blasphemous gods coiled and screamed between the stars. Mortals came into the world as the eons yawned, and through them countless powers rose and fell and rose again.

The pure forms of nature, and time, and the ineffable echoes of life itself became altered. The races, as they are called, became more diverse. New kinds of beasts and even abominations tasted the crisp air of the old woods. The multiplication of all things obscured to most mortals the very existence of the gods, and so, they grew in their rage and lust unchecked.

But the rise of evil made mighty the forces of good, as iron sharpens iron, and they achieved much. So poetry, and valor, and perseverance entered the cosmos.

Millennia later, countless kingdoms had countless stories, and for every wrath unquenched a score more quests met doom or triumph. Dwarves and men endured with their hearts most like those noble beasts of yore, but the more magical souls of elvenkind saw deeper into the dimensions of the universe, and there found darker corruptions and terrible knowledge.

In time, some of their number seethed with resent and age-old feud. Too long had they played the distant scholars and high-chinned watchers. Too long had they abstained from too many of life's little things.

It was these little things that created the Red Captain's hate.

He was a boy, long ago, as happy and care free as any. Son was he to Lenn Furia, Duchess of the Kathic state of Iridess. That part of Kath is wooded with palms and wide fern groves. Theirs was a musical, sunlit place.

He was taught the sword, and the pen. Friends had he on both elbows, and in the open-air courts of Iridess he ran and played war and swam in the crystal waters of the River Isles.

But fate had its eye upon him, and death had stayed silent too long.

It is a matter for scholars exactly how the embalmed dead of the Kathic mages regained their life, but it was common enough that their tombs were barred, locked, and trapped. The dead were revered, even worshipped, but never welcome. For when reanimated they carried a terrible rage and lust for blood that could not be quenched by anything but fiery annihilation.

The bars of Duchess Furia's family tomb rattled that fateful morning, and the Red Captain, a boy of only ten summers, went to look.

His name was Aras unto that day, but never after.

To the tombs he walked, slowing as he approached. He had strayed far from the bright ways of the central court, and riding a wooden drake had come to a part of the city he'd never seen. The metal clanging drew him like the smell of supper.

"Hello?" he squeaked, inching forward toward the high-jambed gate. The sandstone was inlayed with lapis and gold, but he noticed little. In he went and the sun could no longer guard him.

"Hello?" he said again, and again there came no retort. Down a strange cubic hall crept he, bending his neck at the wondrous frescoes that glittered in the dim. At last his steps silenced, and he turned to a barred doorway.

There, standing natural as a height of reeds, was a figure. She was dressed in sheer, golden weaves and green drape. At her neck, a broad, golden gorget wrapped from shoulder to shoulder, held by the most delicate gold chain he'd ever seen. Her face was high and slim, and at her square-cut locks hypnotic, beautiful green eyes shone like emeralds. He let out a gasp, and froze.

"Aras, Lenn's son," she spoke. Her voice echoing from beyond space, the tones rang in his mind and chilled his bones, but it was lovely, and gentle, and musical. "Help me, my love. My time to sleep has ended."

She did not beg, or plead, or move. Her hands stayed at her hips. She was ageless, but young, and glowing with a warm brown sheen on her flawless skin.

Aras could not speak. He realized that for the first time he was feeling true love. It was a white hot, almost painful wanting. He wanted to be held by her, to touch her wide lips, to kill the world for her. Like a spellbound tree he reached out slowly, fixed on her infinite eyes, and set free the glyph-enchanted latch.

She stepped forward. Her bare feet were weightless and perfect. One thumb she placed on his forehead, and again that voice from beyond all worlds vibrated the sandstone like a distant earthquake: "I give you my gift, and go to my red work. Ever will I love you."

When the next moment met Aras' shocked mind, he was sat down on the court steps. Around him the ruin of Iridess burned.

Bodies were piled at the doorways, or skewered on banner poles, or torn apart and strewn like paintbrushes from street to street. Aras was bloodless, pale as a ghost, and unscathed. To his left he looked, catatonic, and there hanged his mother's once exquisite form, now rent and tattered, on the dome-spire of a bubbling fountain. She was stuck from hip to collar bone, and the brass spike glowed with a stream of bright red.

Upon her face he found his eyes horrifically set, unable to look away. She was frozen in her death scream.

None know, least of all him, how long he sat there in madness' grasp, or what had happened. But smoking ruins draw the wrong attention. The city was ransacked, and murmured over, and left to the sands.

The few surviving children of Iridess were traded as slaves, or taken to remote family enclaves. Northmen picked the rubble clean of every brass fitting and iron hinge.

And nothing was done. There was no revenge. There was no rage or kingdom in flames. The town was simply dismantled, and no one spoke of it. Aras found himself in another Duke's care, traumatized. His seething inner hell he could not describe, and none sought to comfort a useless child. So, his madness congealed, and became companion to the sorrow he also knew.

This madness, this despair, drew him back to that crypt years later. A grown man, he delved far further, beyond the deepest chambers of old. There, he found things none know, but when he returned his eyes were infinite green. His bare feet were flawless despite his endless wanderings. His crimson robe was timeless and gleaming with brocades from long-buried kingdoms and ancient secrets.

There was no longer any thought of his childhood, or the happiness he once knew, only the limitless knowledge of the black between the stars, and the gnawing doubt that he had killed them all. The gnawing doubt that he was the demon. The gnawing doubt that all this was illusion and nightmare.

Nevertheless, when nothing was done to avenge his home, there was a hunger for death ignited in him that could not be quelled with reason, for he had none.

"Ever will she love me," he murmured, facing Hannar, Hunnin's son on the pinnacle of the Wall of Duros.

With this, he revealed the obelisk from his cloak, and the power crackled in the air like lightning about to strike.

19

A third skein I now weave into this tale, for without it the end will make little sense. It is well known that both Akram the Falcon, and Hannar, Hunnin's son both met their end fighting back the threat of Manac many years later. Also chronicled are the fates of those countless thousands who lost their lives in the War of the Wall, where elves and dwarves clashed for the birthright of Alfheim. But as the Red Captain sowed the seeds of those tragedies with his campaign of death, little has been spoken of a sword called Angrid.

The primary mention of this artifact is of course on the belt of King Akram, the Sun Stone, as he strode against the Archons and Manac the Cursed. But those events occurred long after the War of the Wall. In any case, history has described the blade as "old as the races" and "bearing an unhewn lodestone at the pommel." These details are all too accurate, but reveal nothing of its origin or weighty significance.

When in pursuit of the Red Captain, and standing beside Elisa the Headsman of Englemoor, Anna, Mars Gulgynn, and the Ramthas Elite; the kind King Akram carried the longhammer of those times. Angrid, the Lawgiver, or Huro Din as it was called by dwarves, was far away. Exactly where it lay is the very linchpin of this tale.

It stood as so many swords do, blade buried 'tween the bust of a giant barmaid. This was a stone effigy of Hela, the dwarven goddess of mirth and truth. Patron goddess of Helmar the lake town was she, and guardian over all the lands from Shipshelm to Gem Glacier. This likeness of her was blocky, rough-hewn, old as time, and leaning with tectonic upheaval.

The gigantic statue sat in geologic silence deep in the bedrock of Duros' lands, far below the great yawning door of legend, and long-lost to myth and cave-ins. Perfect was the inky blackness at those crushing depths, and the mighty sword, all lapis and geodesic etchings of times before the world knew corruption, rested there for eons. By unknown hands it was placed here, and awaited a hand to raise it once more.

This was, by all accounts, the deepest cut chasm in all the world. It was hellishly hot, and so far below the surface was this diamond-shaped chamber that the pressure of the rock above gave any who dared its depths an oppressive, dizzy feeling of fear. All save the true dwarves, who had developed an immunity to such things.

This place was the goal of the Red Captain. His blasphemous visions and war mongering beckoned him here, for his power was forged in the depths, and the deeper he could go, the greater force he could conjure.

His weapon was not the dwarven sword though, but those whipping, barbed, eyeless eels and slapping rubbery tentacles that seethed and twisted in the sewers below Englemoor, and in the woods near Fort Friendship, and everywhere the Red Captain wrought his deadly work. At the world's nave, down in the black, was he beckoned, to summon the true strength of that shapeless god-thing's arm: a tangle of hell to rend the world and pave the way for a dark reign of elvenkind.

In this planting of war-seed was he sanctioned by the royalty of Kath, and the elves of Aphos, and even the woodlings of the Ebon Dim. For they, too, had rotted and pined in the shadow of men and dwarves too long, and left too many wrongs unavenged.

It was a sad truth. And in despair the hideous gods find footholds.

So, they beckoned him there, and he killed all between him and his goal. If he could claim Angrid, the Lawgiver, it would be a collateral boon. If it fell into the abyss it would matter not. No mere steel could stop the slime-wreathed tide of death he meant to conjure.

Now all that stood between the Red Captain, once called Aras of Iridess, was a little boy with a wooden shield. Their clash of wills is one of the greatest battles of that heroic time, and ended with a tragedy that defines this story.

"Ever will she love me," the Red Captain muttered in the high wind of the Wall's upmost rampart. "Ever-"

"You there!" Hannar's voice, not yet deep with adulthood, pierced the cold air like a kestrel call. "You and your troop murdered my father, and scores of others! I'm here to see that you answer for it!" Hannar felt like the voice came from somewhere else. His eyes were hot with pounding beats of his warrior's heart, but he held steady. In his right hand, he held Wall, and in his left the great drifting banner of Duros-Tem.

"Answer?" Aras replied, beginning to shiver but concealing it. "You are just a pup! Your spirit is noted, little fool, now move aside. We've business beyond. Your death is little inconvenience, if you wish it. I remember your father," Aras continued, trying to shake the boy. "I struck him down in one blow, and his friends ran like frightened mice."

The threat was hollow, for biting cold is the ally of dwarves, and these gaunt elven creatures were clearly shaken by the icy gusts. Nevertheless, Hannar was beyond outmatched.

"Then do your worst, villain," Hannar replied unmoved, leaning back and rolling his shoulders. "Surely, you and your skeletons can kill a mere boy with ease. I'm only one, and short as a stump. You have, what, fifty warriors at your neck?"

The Red Captain seethed.

"Go on, then," Hannar taunted, opening and closing his shield fist with a smug grin, "This is a good place to die."

"So eager for death, are you?" and with one wave of the hand the captain called in his fighters. Their kopesh blades flashed from beneath crimson cloaks, and they swarmed around him like rabid wolves closing for a meal. In their eyes, a supernatural glow boiled.

Hannar had hoped that his wild, feral berserker would arise in him, but no such thing happened. He faced the red warriors terrified and alone, wide eyed. But the old blood that made dwarven folk mighty was no fickle thing, and did not let him down. He would battle on pure instinct, and they were the instincts of heroes.

To his left foot he pivoted, crouching back. The banner pole, oak ringed in dull steel and riveted with iron endcaps, he braced at the left toe. The fabric whipped downward, and coiled in the wind between him and his foes. Their vanguard was blinded for a split second, and the twelve-foot pole turned the first three blades akimbo with a clatter. It was already more weight than Hannar could hold, so he let the force spin him like a top.

The banner pole whirled, arriving back at his fore in an instant. A skilled elven fiend there caught the thing with his free hand, and raised his curved blade like an executioner. Hannar, knowing at least a little of dwarven ways, had already planted the pole in a post-hole at the ramparts' stone-seam. It braced, and he lunged forward with Wall as his weapon. The wooden disc met the armpit of the attacker with a cracking thud, and broke the elf's shoulder like a twig. The elf pivoted his weapon to his left hand, though, and finished the attack. The sword ripped through Hannar's vest effortlessly and his blood sprayed in a steaming mist.

At that moment, that weird rage returned. His foolish child's temper unleashed, and across the pave he rolled, springing up and over two foes like a toad. Behind them, he drove Wall into their ankles with a fury. This swept them onto their backs, and he tore one throat from its roots before they could see him wriggling inward.

Then the battle became a messy thing. They were on him in a heap, tangled up, choking and jabbing, and one pommel came down and smote Hannar on the forehead with a wet thud. Blood clouded his eyes. His strength was nowhere near enough to escape. Thoughtless, he lashed forward with teeth bare, and tore an ear free. This broke the deadlock, and he had smashed a groin, broken a few wrists, and brained an enemy in a single heartbeat.

Wall he regained somehow, slid out of the pack, and breathed. They rushed him with foolish anger, and he spun aside. Eight or nine of the ghastly fools slid from the rampart screaming into the open air. It was a long way down.

This drew the ire of the Captain, who was smug no more. He took one step toward the fray, reaching into his cloak with slow menace.

They had pinned Hannar to the center column, all as one they shoved him. There were three elves on each arm and each leg. A terrible pop was heard, and Hannar was immobilized. He was only one boy against half the original force. The mastermind of the elven wars strode forward, glowing with the power of that hideous obelisk. Aloft, like a lantern he carried that fallen star, a crystal fragment of a god from some unimaginable undercavern that stretches into spiral stairways of madness. It was like a scream, and a chorus of wailing angels, and a seismic pressure.

A winding, arcing tendril of pure arcane distortion probed out through the dimensions, through that blasted obelisk, and into the battle-mighty mind of Hannar, Hunnin's son.

It began to do to Hannar what had felled his father: the rise of the whipping things. A cracking, choked death riven and made mockery. Those rows of clawed suckers rose from within, such as the fate of poor Brann in the woods of Fort Friendship. This was now Hannar's fate.

One thing widely known to most of the world, though, is that some dwarves are highly resistant to magic. Hannar held this attribute in the very highest. He was descended of the old elkbeards. He was a child of the boatmen of Helmar and the undefeated raiders of Myron's Bay. Even Akram knew a branch on Hannar's family tree, and it was a proud thing.

Generations of strength, of endurance, of perseverance, and most of all faith; it all gave Hannar a split second longer than his countrymen. The gods were good, for he made great use of that split second.

His strength returned and the dwarf boy jerked his arms free, broke two jaws, then tumbled from his bonds. One sharp stone shard was in his hand, and he hurled it like a jagged missile. The Red Captain was there in plain sight, in some mesmeric fury. The blow was landed, caroming off the obelisk and into the Captain's face.

Aras reeled back, but there were still some twenty elven slashers flying inward toward Hannar. The little dwarf's dire gaze took on that red, arcing fire from beyond time, for a fragment of the obelisks dark power had touched him, and by the wonders that weave our world from the stuff of stars, it made him strong.

Hannar lifted a mighty forearm, and a half-dozen warriors were broken to clatter. Two flew bodily from the wall-top. The rest he dispatched like scattered rats. He broke their swords in his bare hands. He hurled them into pillars and vibrated with terrible power. They were all of them destroyed. Hannar surveyed the carnage of the battle, breathing heavily.

The Red Captain was motionless. He lay on his back, one hand raised. Hannar strode to him in three great leaps. Above the fallen wizard he smoldered, and rose up for the completion of his quest.

But the Red Captain rose casually, almost bored. He looked in Hannar's burning eyes, and the warrior boy froze. He relaxed his pounding shoulders, his heaving elbows. Hannar's gloves fell to the floor with a thump. He let a raspy exhale, and was transfixed by Aras' voice. His strength and rage had perished in the casting, and the spell was complete. The dark mage had taken total control of Hannar's mind at that moment, and if he held on long enough, he would control his very soul.

So it ended. They both stood there, the oddest of couples, now the strangest of companions, and the wind rose again.

"Go," the Red Captain barked at last.

Hannar complied, blank-eyed, and began to work his way down the inner side of the Wall of Duros. It would take most travelers days to descend those heights, but Hannar would find shortcuts that completed the journey in a few hours.

Across the foothills to the great Doors they made haste, and vanished into the snows.

20

The tunnels went on forever.

How they survived the tumbling, sliding, fighting, falling descent from the Wrong Way Tavern is unknown. Mars trailed behind the rest of them, watching every corner, mumbling, smashing the tentacle things when they lurched out from crevasse and sinkhole. O'er his mighty shoulder leaned Ruin, the greatsword he so oddly mastered. It was a wonder to behold, but blocky, almost square-tipped, and with a three-hand hilt that terminated in cubic pommel weights. How he even managed to hold on to it during their fall was a mystery.

And fall they did, well beyond the kiss of sunlight. They stopped at last in the strange, smooth corridors of the undercaverns. This place they had heard of in whispers and speculation, but none had ever dared its depths. There, eleven of them all told, stood in the purplish dim.

Akram held the landing first, checking both routes out of the ledge they smashed into. Then came Kray and six of the Ramthas elite. Anna, Mars and Elisa followed.

"Where are these things coming from?" Akram grumbled, helping Anna adjust her scabbard, "Gods and Devils, look at this place," His kingly voice was gone, and he was in awe of the works of deep creatures.

"Wherever this Red Wizard goes," Anna hissed, pulling her belts away and repairing them herself, "the damned things multiply and kill."

"Then we're on his trail," Elisa answered, uninvited. She took a step toward Anna and Akram. "I am Elisa," she went on, removing her headsman's mask. The tentacle-burns were mostly healed, but it mattered not. The beauty and truth in her wide face put them all at ease.

Some versions of the story say that the Falcon fluttered at the sight of her. In any case, our greatest King, the Sun Stone, was speechless before her in her full revelation.

"My King," she began again, softening her shoulders, lowering her knotted hands. She was feminine as a waving reed and yet thick as an oak. "I tried to fight them back... the entire town... we fought together."

Akram said nothing, but glowed at her with gratitude. Here stood valor incarnate.

"What I mean to say is," she continued after a pause, "yours are a mighty people, my lord." At Akram's feet she bent her wondrous form, on one knee loyal as the mountains. Her broad back spread the motley scraps of leather and mail, and every warrior there gasped. She was exquisite.

"Rise," Akram said gently. He was the kind of king that could say that, and make you an instant friend. This came naturally to those of the old blood.

"Our fight was not lost, my King," Elisa went on, lifting her chin and meeting his gaze. "We cornered the devilish whips in one street. The entire guard was at my side, and folk rose up..." She paused and felt awkward, "Gah! I've no talent for oratory. They fought bravely, the folk of Englemoor, and we destroyed most of its number, and tracked it."

Akram smiled, and nodded, and let her finish.

"They seem to appear eastward, some scouts say even beyond Duros-Tem and the Wall." Elisa had been fighting these things for days. She was hungry as a devil, and could barely rise from her knee.

"We follow these whips," Akram took up, "for where they are, the Red Captain will be. To find him is to find Hannar, and so we go."

"Yes, my King. First we eat," Anna stepped forward and offered one arm up to Elisa, who was three heads taller. The two women took arms, and braced, and smiled with those lips that only women can use to smile. The moment broke, and the dead were remembered with solemn names over cold tomatoes and pemmican.

They were alive. Deep in some hellish tunnel melted clean by a wriggling primordial wyrm, but alive.

"You're quite a fighter," Kray finally uttered, breaking the mood again. He was small and knobby like a camel, but older than Elisa and battle-worn. He leaned on his hammer, still chewing, "You must be Elisa, Fenn's little girl..."

Elisa was speechless.

"He was a great rider," Kray went on, wistfully. "It's too bad what happened."

"Nurin's folk crave a good death," she answered with subtext.

"Aye," Kray confirmed, leaning back to rest on the smooth stone. It was hot, and echoing, and to be down there was at once wondrous and horrific. But, they were together, and they smiled. Elisa's stare lingered on Kray a moment too long, and she cracked her knuckles to distract herself.

"So, we head east through this blasted tunnel network?" Kray tied his hammer-belt anew.

"Aye," Akram confirmed casually, "folk say the undercaverns go on for miles, though I never wanted to find out personally. Every one of us is beat to bruises and nursing a million burning bites."

Little was said, but as the eleven of them went quiet, leaning against the weird, smooth walls, a friendship took root. Like wolves burrowing in winter they now knew that trust of those who have only each other, and when it came time to rise, and tighten down boots, and begin walking, they trudged ahead more as a family than a band of survivors.

Still, Mars trailed behind. He took no comfort in company. His mind was set like an arrow on Hannar. He owed it to Hunnin to find the boy, and make him safe, no matter what it took.

He meant to do exactly that.

So, they walked.

For six days, or what they guessed to be days, they walked. The undercaverns bent and spiraled, or broke into jagged pockets and hellish ledges. The abyss was always there, through narrow sinkholes, running waterfalls, or weird bulbous throats of bottomless limestone. They ate like birds, burned bits of cloth for light, and huddled in uncertain horror to rest. It was an ordeal beyond the sanity of most, but this was no rabble. These were the finest warriors in the realm, and one worried mother.

Oft times Anna led the group. The love of a mother is no small thing, and can carry the weight of the Urth even in the blackest doom.

"I can smell them," Anna said, stepping carefully on pillar-like blobs of purplish bedrock. "We're on the trail now for sure… getting closer."

Elisa crouched down. The ceiling dripped on her massive shoulders, and she glistened with scrapes and cuts, "Scratch marks here… boots."

They kept moving, and Mars at last passed the same place, "These are no dwarven iron toes," he huffed. "Those are the pointy cleats of an elven brigade."

"How do all the pieces fit together?" the good King Akram continued, pausing with one arm on a wet wall, "A marauding sorcerer, new hells from the deep, and elves in his employ, but why?"

"War, my King," Kray said. It was the first he had spoken since the day they landed in the caves. Normally, he and the elite stayed almost silent, holding an incredible and deadly discipline that stemmed from their love of the King. "The elves have pined too long at the fringe of the Greenway, as you know all too well, my King."

Akram's mighty head fell to his chest, his etched helm catching the faint torchlight from Anna's lead. He knew Kray was right, but the thought of it pained him. The elves would be outmatched, for theirs had been a dark road, and public opinion had turned against them. The number among them that still held true to old ways was few indeed, though they were not yet seen as villains.

"The people of Ramthas will be ready, and with them all the folk of the Alfheim." Akram lifted his gentle gaze, and managed a smile for Kray.

"Elisa," Kray turned, "you and Mars have seen more of this devilry than any of us... What is the connection between the elf-fiends and the Red Captain? What are we hunting?"

Mars jumped in, resting Ruin's massive blade and taking a knee. "They are his weapon, and a foul one at that. I've never seen elves fight like this, with undeath at their left hand, and conjuring these poisonous whips on the right. He means to kill until a reprisal is unavoidable, and pull all the lands east of Koab into some deadly play for the Greenway and all of the lands of Duros."

"Why Duros?" Elisa asked, knowing of the massive dwarven kingdom but never seeing it with her own eyes.

"It is the largest defensible place in Alfheim. These tunnels seem to lead us ever closer to the Wall, where that mass of bedrock will force us up. If I had to guess, I'd say he seeks some deep place to conjure the mother of these infernal snakes, and destroy Duros from within."

"All that from a trail of slime in a cave," Anna smiled, breaking the mood. She was gifted with unending hope, and in these conditions, it was a survival skill. Optimism was their weapon, and they would cling to it with white-knuckled certainty.

"I have warred against this Red Captain," Mars went on, "and I met his eyes at Fort Friendship, when that red lightning crackled out and struck down good Hunnin. I met the fiend's eyes and saw his pathetic plan, his wounded soul, his self-righteous delusion."

"But, do the elven kingdoms back him," Akram asked in a stately tone. "If not, his war will end the day we find him."

This vow brought Mars to his feet, and he remembered who was King once again, and it was a good feeling.

"My King," a whisper came from the elite ranks, then a gloved hand raised in fist. This was the signal for silence, and danger. The grouped hushed, and tensed. Kray took the cue, followed his compatriot's eyeline, and spotted movement in the ink-black tunnels ahead. He gestured to hold post, and crept forward like a panther.

The silent warrior vanished into the dark, and Elisa was uneasy. She was unarmed. The headsman's giant axe and the ghoulish hood from her exile were long gone. Now she sported a ringmail skirt, rolled boots, a leather halter, and knuckles wrapped in cotton belts like a pit fighter.

A long moment passed in pure suspense. No one breathed.

Then with a crash, Kray came flying out of the black like a missile, bent forward but flying backward. He hurtled toward the wall behind the group, which was all jagged and broken stone. Only Elisa was in any position to react, so sudden was

Kray's flight across the chamber. She ducked to one side like a deep-stanced monk. Her speed was remarkable.

Into Elisa's chiseled stomach flew he, and slammed into her bodily. Despite her massive bulk, easily two heads taller than the ring-clad warrior of Ramthas, she was pushed utterly into that rocky wall with terrible force, and knocked senseless and winded. Kray remained unharmed and caught his feet at her side.

There wasn't a moment to react, for it then revealed itself: what was once an elf, but swollen with mass and pale as snow. At its high grey forehead, a burn mark glistened, gleaming red, and Mars recognized that fell scar. It was the fate of Brann, and Hunnin. This elf-thing had been obelisk-touched, and the whips began to split open its ribs, and sprout from each arm like massive cobras writhing up to kill.

The entire group locked eyes with the monster, and charged forth. Even Anna lunged forward, raising her dagger in a reverse grip.

Kray, though, spun, and surveyed poor Elisa, who was unconscious, and had coughed a mouthful of crimson onto her lovely chin. This he wiped clean, and her face, even in such a peril, was glowing and wondrous at that close distance. Her wide eyes and square jaw reminded him of the old statues of Aphos, but greater, for she held a kindness in her lips and eyebrows that no empty-eyed god's image could ever have.

He managed both his arms under hers, and went to lift her, hoping to help her regain her wind, but gods, she was heavy as an ox and he fumbled.

"Hells, woman, are you made of stone?" he muttered, bracing to try again. But he did not get the chance, for the battle with that eel-twisted elf-thing took a destructive turn.

Akram, Mars, Anna, and the elite all circled the creature, hacking at flying tentacles and wrestling barbed-suckers in a chaotic fray. The good King raised his hammer, but feinted that blow and spun reverse with a backhand arc. The weapon landed handily, upending the convulsing thing. When it hit, the stone floor a split second later, the impact jarred some hideous rage loose, and it let out an otherworldly howl of sonic fury. One massive, slime-coated black whip then spiraled up from the torso, tearing it apart utterly. This eel-like column of muscle was as thick as an elephant, and spun with frightening speed.

It lashed like a rubber lightning bolt across the space between them, slamming into the stone walls near Elisa and Kray. A deep, groaning crack was heard, and the chamber simply crumbled.

Boulders rained down from above, the floor opened and vanished, and they all scrambled for grip on something, anything, to survive. All those at the fore managed this, for that part of the cavern less smote, but at the rear the entire wall gave way and slid straight down into the abyss, taking Kray and Elisa with it. They vanished in a roar of tumbling rubble, plummeting down into some hellish depth where any impact was drowned by distance and calamity.

21

A long conversation with a hillwoman is no small thing.

They're stubborn folk, with little patience for talk. This particular conversation was compulsory, though, considering Kray and Elisa were jammed into a limestone shaft fifty feet straight down, and barely alive.

They heard struggle and clatter far above. Yells and grunts followed, then a long unnerving quiet. They would find a way to reach their comrades above.

In the meantime, the two were squeezed chest-to-chest in the vertical opening, with barely room to inhale or move their arms. Elisa, much larger, was still unconscious, and had taken a nasty blow to the head on the way down. Kray was stuck a bit higher than her, so his chin was at her forehead, and he had one broken arm. It throbbed and stung like mad, as it was pinned between him and the slimy flowstone.

"Quite a fix we've landed in here, eh?" he mused, knowing she would not answer, but believing she could hear. "I was hoping we could get some time alone."

Kray was a lean, wiry fighter, and no older than thirty. He was muscular, but fast, and handsome in a simple way. His skin was mocha, with a week of stubble to lend gravity to those dark brown eyes. His was simple blood from the farm folk of the Greenway. He managed a smile, winced, and got his left arm free. The fingers were scratched to hell, and his gloves were shredded, but no broken bones on that side.

With this ragged hand, he gently touched Elisa's beautiful cheek. Was it to wake her, soothe her, or just out of his own affection for her? She was easy to love, and this man had nothing to fear. He touched again.

At that, she awoke with a start, staring upward into his face, now glowing. She tried to recoil from his touch, but there was no room, and she hit her head again. That sent a wave of black through her eyes and she almost passed out again.

"Easy does it," Kray soothed, withdrawing the hand. "No sudden movements, eh?"

"What-where are we?"

"All hell broke loose up there. We took a dive down to this cozy little getaway. I suppose they'll try to get a rope down."

"Attacked... we... what was that?"

"Another of the fiends," he didn't want to remember it. "Some kind of elf warrior, but all filled up with those eyeless snakes. Gods, what a day."

She chuckled, but it hurt, and she blinked at him. Time froze, and Kray saw a moment. He leaned forward to kiss her.

"What are you doing?" Elisa barked, trying to pull back, interrupting the rapture. Kray was rugged, and unafraid of her, and his eyes were filled with honesty and affection. She did not like how that made her feel. "Now? We're half dead in a bottomless crack and you're getting romantic?"

Kray paused, considered the answers, and leaned in again. This time fast, and managed a kiss before she could feign her horror at it.

"If I'm to die down here, I wanted to get that done." He smiled wide and they both relaxed, laughing in spite of themselves.

"Not a word," she said.

"To my grave," he answered.

They kissed again, and he held her neck gently. It helped with the pain.

"So," Kray continued, elated with his new conquest, "tell me of your home, Headsman."

"You're pretty proud of yourself, eh runt?" she snorted back. One big inhale and she could crush the man. Her collar bones were as wide as his shoulders, and her skin somehow gleamed flawless and smooth in the muck and dripping cave slime.

"I mean it. Where do you come from? We seem to have the time."

"The hills, of course. My marriage went awry in Englemoor, to say the least, and anger got the better of me. I've no stories to tell or poetry for you and your doe eyes."

"Marriage?"

"Don't worry, dreamer, it ended before it began, and I chose exile over a life of slavery to some mewling whelp."

"I can't imagine the fate of the poor soul that tried to tame your wild heart," he gently moved her blonde hair from the wound on her head, and managed a bit of cloth to clean the scrape.

"My hips are killing me," she commented. "Jammed on some pointy pebble down there."

"There's nothing for it, I can't move a muscle and my arm must be cracked in two."

She could see the arm, just a glimpse. It was purple, and bent awfully. The man must've been in agony, and still he smiled at her like a teenage schoolboy at his first brothel.

"I guess I don't have to warn you to keep your hands to yourself." They laughed a little, and it hurt a lot.

"So, why all this?" Kray asked. "Why this resolve to pursue these monsters?"

"Evil grows, dark times loom. Someone must act, so I act. Besides, our King stands at the helm, you expect me to cry and go home?"

"Hardly. More like join the elite. We could use a fighter like you. Hells, you'd probably be captain within a week."

"You go ahead," she saw the detail in his face when he blinked. He was a noble and brave man, born of the blood that cut Ramthas rock from its roots. She felt a feeling stir, and quashed it immediately with a huff. "I've no use for goose stepping and suitors."

"And I none for a frozen heart..." They paused, smiled again, and that one got her. She grinned into a gentle, lovely giggle. Few men, if any, could ever speak to her in such a way. She had blocked herself away in battle and high-chinned pride. But here he was, this little runt, and he spoke to her with no lust, or insult, or terror.

The broken bones took their toll, and Kray's eyes rolled in his head. He gulped, squinted away the pain, then passed out. His head flopped forward.

"Kray?" Elisa asked, a touch of worry in her voice, "Kray?"

Only the silence of that deep, shadowy hell answered. There was no sound above, and the unnatural heat of the womb of the world was cloying. Elisa looked up, wincing with the motion of her sprained neck, and no hint of the others betrayed the gloom. Were the rest even alive? Would the eels descend at any second to tear them both apart? Would they simply starve here? She pictured two pathetic skeletons jammed into a rock shaft for eons. That image she shook away, and the fury of the Headsman returned. She wiggled a finger, and determined herself to survive.

22

"This tavern began as many do," Gus huffed from the wall of bottles, "when a goat gave birth to a donkey on the autumn equinox." It was cold that night, blowing snow, one lonely lantern lit the wooden dim, and only garrison dwarves were at the cups. Gus Elmer's son tended the bar.

"That's a load of manure, you old fish," one patron mumbled, face and beard buried in a wooden mug. Foam crackled at his red moustache. All three drinkers were stout as trees, short as stumps, and crusted with melting snow. The guard of Duros were a hearty lot, but even they took a chill this night.

"Aye," Gus went on, unfazed. He washed one tall glass goblet with a rag as old as time, and his apron was crispy clean against his braided beard. "An omen of the nobler gods it was, and the spot was marked by the Gulgynns, and the even the kin of Phram the Berserk."

"Phram wasn't even a real person! That was a whole brigade of spears went by that nickname."

"I heard this shanty was begun as a latrine for the old wall builders. Tired of walking from mugs to ditch, they combined the sites!" At this, a chuckle came, and mugs were knocked like bells. Gus relented and returned the goblet to its rack with care.

The Foamy Goat some called that place, but its official name was Rinn's Rest. It lay in the frigid high foothills between the Wall of Duros and the great Doors, which served as the entrance to the Undermountain realm of all the Dwarves and their true-blood kinfolk. The tavern was a sort of waystation for garrison guards moving back and forth to posts, wagoning supplies or on repair detail. Those old timbered walls had stood for five generations. That was almost fifteen hundred years by dwarven count, and they showed the wear. Every corner was worn, every table replaced a dozen times over, every floor board worn to tatters and scarred with brawls and dance. A massive moose head, wide as the room itself, spanned the length of the bar, and from its mighty antlers hung daggers, gold chains, and baubles of all kinds from over the years. It was a good place. The kind of place worth fighting for in those times.

But this was the last night any dwarf would taste Gar there, the last night those noble old timbers would stand.

Now, on the note of Gar, Gus stocked a half-dozen taps most days, filling the frontmost barrels with a black stout for breakfast. No mug is as crucial to dwarven disposition as breakfast. Behind these he kept two reds; one with a hoppy tang, almost like cider, and the other a flat, room temperature swill fit for those already drunk. Finally, there was the gold. This recipe Gus brewed himself in the ancient cellars, and took great pride in it. It was called Queen's Kiss by most, or Liquid Sunshine. A gold piece for a single mug, it was held as one of the finest ales in all history. Tonight, the four of them were at the hoppy red. Red Gar can make a fierce hero of a dwarf.

"Tell me again," one guard murmured, at his mug, "when we make for the Doors? I've a hankerin' for home."

"Three nights hence," his companion answered. "The Undermountain is all but empty with the brigades bolstering in the South. We've a lot of ground to cover."

"Blasted elven liars," the third soldier grunted, "Why don't they just declare war and make their move? All this subterfuge is a waste of time."

Gus surveyed this conversation, well aware of the brewing conflict with the elves. A new generation of warriors among them was rising in popularity, and they sought to restore what they once had held and lost. It was only a matter of time.

"You'll get your war soon enough, clodbrain," he punctuated, "and only a fool wishes for a tide of death."

The soldier rose suddenly, kicking his stool backward, fuming.

"He's right," the first guard barked. "Itching for a fight and an all-out war are two very different things."

The standing soldier huffed, knocked back a heroic quaff of the spicy ale with a splash, and slammed the mug down. "You're right, lads," he admitted. "It's not war or death I crave, just a good knock on the helmet."

The middle guard obliged, clocking him square with his mug. The dwarf bounced backward, forgetting his stool was gone, and flopped onto the planked floor like an upended wagon. He froze, wide-eyed, then burst out laughing.

"Another round, Gus! And pour like you mean it!" At this, a cheer came to the quiet tavern, and the wind answered.

No one knows exactly how it happened, for snow and distance kept hidden the actual events of that night, and no dwarf lived to tell the tale.

The Red Captain took refuge there from the night's bluster, en route to the Doors of Duros. At his side went Hannar, struggling against the dark power that kept his will in the Red Captain's control. He must have been a grim sight after the battle atop the Great Wall, a headlong sprint across the frigid foothills, and finally standing there in the entrance to Rinn's Rest tavern.

Legends tell of the woe that young dwarf endured that dark night. Made the hellish weapon of black magic, joining forces with the very target of his wrath, made to kill his own folk. This woe took its toll on him, and aged were his eyes beyond their short years. They glowed like demonfire, and in that gaze the sadness of eons unfairly burned.

History knows only what scene was found by Akram's company, days later. They had recovered Kray and Elisa from their rocky throat and wandered through the tunnels of solid rock, finally emerging at the ruined garrison of Kellan. From there, they crossed the mighty Wall of Duros, and made chase across the frigid foothills. Up to Rinn's Rest, the Foamy Goat called by some, they walked with horror in their guts. No smoke spiraled up from the building, it was silent and dark. Snow licked at its blocky roof, a one-sided A-frame style with three high gables and a massive central joist beam that stood broad and ancient at each end. On each wall, three high windows yawned, unbroken, but black as cavern shadows. The wind hummed and turned. It was late morning, and Akram hesitated. In his heart, he knew a great darkness lay here, and it pained his brow.

In through the iron-rimmed door they stepped, slowly, like thieves in a tomb. Akram was at the lead, longhammer in hand, his brass helmet adorned with those triangular plates and chevrons of his time. His great clasped beard waved with the breeze, and his shoulders held a mighty wolf pelt.

Next was Elisa, the Headsman of Englemoor, who sported little to stave off the cold. Her flawless skin defied the ice, and was beautiful. She towered above the Falcon King like a giant, but her lovely features were placid and calm. Her great axe lost in the caves, she sported ringmail and, now, a half-dozen salvaged swords and hand pikes from fallen foes and cobwebbed caches found since.

Then came Kray, the warrior of Ramthas, in mail and tunic. His chiseled scruff was shadowed by his silver helm. One hand he lay on Elisa's shoulder, for he nursed three broken ribs, a broken arm, and countless scratches and bruises from his fall in the undercavern. With him walked Anna, Hannar's mother, who was no soldier but had the look of a seasoned traveler. She was wrapped in a thick gray cloak, fur at the hood and clasped with an iron clip. In her eyes the deepest fear gathered, for she knew at once her son had been here.

Behind her followed what remained of the Elite. These warriors now numbered six in all, their numbers thinned by that elven horror in the under realm. They were grim, and silent, and mimicked every footstep of Kray as they approached. All of them entered the tavern without sound, surveying the scene, aghast.

And finally came Mars Gulgynn. The snow gathered at his beard in clumps, his eyes were burning with anger. He had buried enough of his kin to last a lifetime, and his stomach knew more dead awaited them here. Over one shoulder he carried Ruin, the famed blade of his age. It was broad and blue with cold danger, reflecting the grays and reds of his beard and helm. He knew nothing of stealth, and clumped onto the wooden floor without care. There was little left to lose.

"Gus!" Mars barked suddenly, breaking the gloomy silence and making Kray flinch. "Gus!" Mars shoved his way forward carelessly, stomping across the tavern to the bar.

The place was all in shambles: overturned tables, shattered chairs, and wall shelves torn to pieces. Weapon marks and splintered planks accented every corner. Gus, that age-old barman Mars had known so well in his early days, lay face down at his station.

"No..." Mars trailed off, reaching the bar in terror. Gus' face had been mashed into the bartop with terrible force. Splinters and cracks in the wood radiated out from his crushed skull like a crater. Nearby, in pools of dried blood, three more dwarves lay dead. One was missing an arm, where it had been torn out by the roots. Another was bent horribly backward over a handrail, eyes wide open in death's final second. The cold had made them all rigid, for they had been there for days.

"They show no mark of the obelisk," Akram spoke solidly, moving from one to the next.

"That's because the Red Captain did not kill these good folk," Anna replied from nearby, "my son did." In her hands, she held a splinter of wood. It was unremarkable to most, but Mars recognized it immediately. It was a mushy, pitted piece of pine mended with makeshift iron strips and a rusted nail. Anna knew every dimple and grain line of that fragment. It was a piece of Wall. She had extracted it from Gus' smashed skull. She began to cry.

"We don't know that," Mars answered, refusing to imagine it.

"We're gaining on them, my King," Kray interrupted. He stooped, with a wince, to the hearth. It was not warm, but had not iced over or gone soggy. Its last fire was only three or four days distant. To Anna the Falcon walked, gently holding up one great broad and gloveless hand. This he placed on hers, and looked into her tear-filled eyes. She was drawn and bloodless.

"We do not rest until that demon is destroyed, and your son restored," Akram said with that stately tone that stirred heroes' hearts. "This I swear by all the old blood, by Udin's eye and Thoor's hammer. War be damned, they've made a boy into a killer..."

Anna fell into his arms and wept. All of them, a haggard, battered company, stood in silence and waited. But Anna was still a dwarf maiden, and strong as a bear. She took a breath, and rose. Into each face she then peered, and made stiff her chin against the dread.

"We go no further until these noble dwarves lay in the stones the old way," she said. "Will you help me?" No words were uttered, but all eleven of them worked together and finished the grim work in silence.

A dwarven funeral is no small thing. But this day, late in the morning at Rinn's Rest, there were no songs, or vows, or mighty stones stood on end. Cairns stood noble and lonely in the snows, the doors were closed, and a lone black banner whipped at the roof's crest as they continued onward to the east. Their tracks were wiped away by the wind, and like a terrible mausoleum the tavern slowly diminished into the horizon behind them.

On the last ridge, with the Foamy Goat almost out of view, Mars Gulgynn tarried. Like an ancient granite statue he stood, sword straight down, and lowered his head. He could not shake the nightmare forming in his mind: that Hannar would stand 'tween them and their prey. He remembered guzzling Gar with old Gus, and his own brother Brann torn limb from limb and cut down by Ruin's unfailing edge. Every drop of dwarven blood he would take back from the Red Captain.

He lifted his chin, and as he stared into the distance the wind rose, and the blowing snow hid Rinn's Rest from view. It is good that none of his company saw his face at that moment, for all the fury of his folk was on him, and nobility was burned away by vengeance. There was no war to avert, no mystery to solve, no wrongs to make right, only a life to end on Ruin's thirsty blade.

23

The clock of existence ticks ahead at the strangest moments. The eons yawn and turn in impossible scale around us, but we never seem to notice the ending of an epoch until it has long since passed. New generations rise and fall, but only looking back are those crucial turning points made clear.

All the efforts of the ineffable gods go like rain on a rooftop, and the lives of countless mortals flow over the centuries like blood on a battlefield. Behind time and between dimensions the true essence of it all goes hidden and unwavering as we live and die.

The luxury of the tale-teller is to know those monumental markers of time, and make good on them for a yarn that will endure. So it was that such a moment came to Alfheim, the fourth realm of Urth, when a lonely gleam of torchlight fell on the flawless, rune-etched surface of Angrid, the Lawgiver, or Huro Din as it was called by dwarves.

This light, barely there and oppressed by crushing blackness, grew. A crack crumbled in a far wall, and for the first time in countless centuries, light betrayed the lightless fathoms of the diamond-shaped chamber. Its ceiling was a hundred feet beyond the ridge-carved floor, and at one end stood the leaning effigy of Hela, half that height. The fissure widened, allowing more light, and two forms were revealed against the gloomy orange glow. A cloaked gaunt figure stepped through the fracture, hands hidden, followed by a dwarven boy holding a flickering flame in one hand, and a withered wooden shield in the other. Clad in tatters and studded belt was the boy, and his brow was twisted with grim resistance to the dark wizard's supernatural will.

These were Aras, the Red Captain, Herald of the Devourer, dwarf-bane, and Hannar Hunnin's son.

Through the last bit of rubble Hannar kicked his way, and they crossed that eldritch place with silent awe. Beside the great towering statue of Hela there was a sort of jagged outcrop. Some seismic shock had shaken the room in ages past, leaning the statue to one side and opening a bottomless abyss below. At the precipice of this unfathomable drop the rock face jutted outward, and the Red Captain knew this was the deep place that had beckoned him. The Devourer would rise here, rise and multiply and shatter the stone above to reveal itself to the doomed world. Their journey had been aided by magicks, and controlling the mighty mind of Hannar was also taxing, so the wizard needed rest before the great ritual. They sat there at Hela's stone feet.

Two days passed they there in Hela's chamber. At last, the Red Captain's power was gathered, so he rose.

"No doubt, our enemies give chase, boy," Aras began. Mortal voices in that hell-deep chamber were unnatural and unwelcome. "Arm yourself with a true weapon, will you?" With this he gestured upward.

There above them, in the very bust of Hela, rested a dwarven sword. Hannar, unable to resist the bidding of his arcane master, ascended the statue with blank eyes. He reached out, trembling, and grasped the hilt of that artifact. Even in his clouded state, Hannar knew the weight of this moment. The sword drew out from its perch, and the ringing was long and harmonic like a tuning fork. The steel was flawless, its balance perfect, the edge like a timeless razor. The folds were infinite in the reflective perfection. Lawgiver. Angrid, the King's Blade, Huro Din. The great heirloom of all dwarvenkind.

Then stood Hannar facing the makeshift entrance. He held the legendary sword in his left hand, and Wall in his right. Like a stone golem, he was motionless, on guard, and grim-faced as death itself.

Aras, the Red Captain threw his cloak back, revealed that blasphemous obelisk, and scampered atop the outcrop with a gulp. The vast black was all around him. Like a demigod he held out his arms, and began to speak the dead words taught him from the cold of space. The Devourer was near, and the journey at an end. They had passed through the great Doors, and moved through the abandoned reaches of the Undermountain undetected. The dwarf realms were all but empty in those days, and it was a silent lonely place.

A humming, a rumbling, and whispering of inhuman tongues. The end of the world began, but by heroic effort, hearts pounding, feet in shreds, eyes sleepless and weary, King Akram and his company made their appearance. One by one they crept into the chamber, facing off with Hannar. All the mortal realm lay in the balance. The Red Captain knew they had come, but acknowledged them not and continued. His dire servant would take care of these insects. The chanting rolled on.

"Hannar!" Anna cried, stumbling in through the crumbling crack. "It's over son." But she hesitated. His face was blank, and he recognized no one. Slowly his shield and sword raised. "Hannar, hear me my little tiger... Hannar?"

Akram sensed what was happening, and strode forth in front of Anna. He held a broad open hand ahead of him, cautious, but hoping to disarm the boy. His other clasped his hammer, and the Elite took their cue.

"Stay where you stand," Hannar spoke in a ringing, phased demonic voice from beyond this world. "Stay and witness the Devourer."

Akram meant to subdue him. The Red Captain was in view, but fifty feet away and would not be easy to reach. Only a heroic throw of a weapon could make contact at that range, and a miss meant one less blade in the battle to come.

"Stay... where... you.... STAND!" With this, Hannar's eyes lit with pinkish fire, and he opened his chest to brandish arms. Then together he slammed Angrid and Wall, taking one lunging step toward Akram and his company. They flinched at this terrible sight, and Hannar used their hesitation to unleash hell.

Angrid sang through the air with a flash, and Akram met the attack with his hammer, parrying. The force of the blow was beyond possible. Akram's iron boots splintered the basalt floor with a crack, and his hammer was pushed back into his face. The clang still rung out as Hannar's next attack unfolded. He opened his right arm, still crushing Akram with his left, and knocked Hauser aside as the Elite guard charged in. The force of this blow was terrible, and Hauser slid like a doll into the far pillar, hitting it with a horrible crack of bone.

Anna stumbled backward, and Elisa joined the fray with fury. She reached forward to grapple the raging boy, but he pivoted to one knee, and twisted Akram into a tumble. Wall he raised, deflecting Elisa's massive gloved hands. From there he turned to the opposite hip, lowering his head. Angrid spun around with a lapis flash and met its mark on Elisa's left leg, cleaving through boot and flesh. She fell, but caught herself with one hand and drew a shortsword with the other.

"Hannar! Stop!" Anna cried out, but she was spellbound and shocked, paralyzed with terror. The Elite lurched forward, attacking in unison. They covered Hannar like a swarm of beetles, but then exploded away from him. The boy was mighty with arcane power, and the soldiers flew in all directions. Two of them clattered and slid into the abyss near the great outcrop, and their screams faded into the endless black.

This Hannar used to take the initiative, and shot forward like a missile. Angrid before him, he skewered one of the surviving Elite utterly. They had no chance against him. Another he crushed into pulp with Wall, and the shield buckled. It was little more than splinters and iron bands now, but the little berserk fought on like a crazed animal.

Mars brought forth Ruin's awful blade, and it met Angrid with a hail of sparks. Impossibly, Hannar parried, braced, and rebounded the blow sending Mars reeling back. Ruin hit the floor with a screech of steel on stone.

At that moment, some mythic power vibrated through the walls, through the very roots of the earth, and an arc of glowing hellfire flashed in a blinding tendril of light. The Red Captain let a cry, and stood at the epicenter of the energy, now rapturous and bathed in spirals of dancing ember.

This hell's-light glowed brighter now in Hannar's eyes, but as he turned to engage Akram again, Kray found his strength.

He slid on one hip across the fray, evading Elisa and Mars, who had re-engaged the boy. At Hannar's side was he then, and his longhammer shot out like a spear. The haft tangled into Hannar's right arm, between him and Wall. Kray braced, ducked, then leapt overhead like a pole vaulter. The length of his hammer twisted into Hannar's elbow with a weird leverage, and Wall was cast free of the boy's grasp, landing twenty paces away with a bang. Kray found his feet, but Hannar tracked his movement with empty eyes and brought Angrid to bear.

The lapis-etched sword met its mark, and cut Kray from stomach to sternum. The wound was shallow, but terribly ragged. Kray sprawled, just as Elisa brought another blow. Her sword shattered on Hannar's back like a twig on a rock. At this, she stared wide-eyed.

Her pause gave Hannar a tiny window, and he reached up to her. His hand barely reached her neck, but with a little leap he made the mark, and crushed her throat in his empty hand. Landing, he pulled her down by the neck, and her face turned purple with strain and airless agony. Akram rushed in, locking up the boy's sword arm, and Ruin came down on Angrid with a great glowing arc of steel, disarming the boy.

But their hopes were dashed as fast as they had been raised. Disarmed entirely, Hannar seemed unfazed. He cast Akram off like a nuisance, knocking the King's helm into the black chasm. An arc of reddish lightning jerked and flashed from the Red Captain to Hannar, renewing his power again. Elisa he twisted and flung like a ragdoll. Her massive, chiseled frame tumbled across the room with crippling force, knocked senseless. Then Mars was kicked in the chest, and slid backward. The boy was unbeatable!

"Release him, demon!" Anna screamed, but the din of rumbling death and otherworldly power was louder than any earthly noise. The Red Captain's arms were raised, and raw power arced and flashed all around him, connecting the abyss, the walls, Hannar, and the wizard himself in a webwork of white-hot plasma.

Akram surveyed the battle like a general. Elisa was unconscious, the Elite lay dead. Kray was barely able to stand, and Mars slowly rose to wage another strike. There was simply no way around the boy to stop the wizard from his hideous work. So Akram, the Sun Stone, set his toes, and eyed his only hope: Angrid. The blade lay to his left, Hannar was at his right. He ducked, feinted, and as Mars came flying in with Ruin on high, the King made for the sword.

In his regal hand that blade rose, and he joined the fight again. This time he made for a crippling cut at the boy's boots, but the strike bounced away. Ruin had Hannar tangled for a moment, but then Hannar broke Mars' hand with sheer force and had the warrior at his mercy. Akram struck again like thunder, but such was the enchantment upon Hannar that it had little effect.

No words of bards or jesters will ever truly capture how terrible was that melee...

The beam of energy that connected Hannar and the Red Captain intensified, and he began to totally overpower the two dwarves with blazing fury. Then happened something that will be told of for all time: Anna, shieldmaiden of the Greenway, found her courage, and strode forth.

She took up Wall, bracing her arm into what was left of the leather grips, took three great running strides, and skidded to a halt at her goal. Between the Red Captain and Hannar she stood, and raised Wall like a great blockade. This brought her directly into the river of fire that gave Hannar his demonic might, and the energy met Wall with a crackling flash of death. Her hair caught fire, her left arm was burnt skinless in an instant, and she screamed.

"Release himmmm!" she howled. Bits of metal, bone, and molten flesh sprayed around her, but the beam was broken. Into her feet she leaned with strength known only to the immortals who first walked the world, and held fast. The shield was ripped to dust, and she held her hands up in the lightning. In a split second her arms were skeletal things, fingers tearing away like ashes in a storm.

With this Hannar stumbled forward, and the fury left him. He smoldered, and fell to his knees. Akram and Mars were set free from their grapple. They shook off the pain of a dozen cracked bones. Akram used Angrid to lift his weight and face the scene, horrified. Mars struggled to focus his eyes, and was still trying to catch his breath.

This was a defining moment, when a king is made legend. For, unafraid and without wrath, he stepped forward and raised that terrible sword like a beacon. Into the blinding arc of energy he lunged, at Anna's side. The sword deflected the demonic power into scattered refractions of death, but it was beyond too late. Anna was no more.

The glowing wreckage of her form crumpled backward, armless, with little more than a cinder where her noble head once was. This at last drew the ire of Aras, the red wizard of Iridess. He turned at his rocky perch, eyes blazing and voice like a dire god. Some terrible force was he readying to unleash, but Mars was the faster of them, and meant to make this moment count.

The dwarf blasted forward with a wild howl, past Akram, past the ashen corpse of Anna, wife to his closest friend, and as Hela looked on from her stone effigy, he made good on his heroic blood. Ruin he brought up like a lance, and there was no stopping him. The blade shot forward, upward, outward. At the tip of that rocky knife he skewered the Red Captain like a boar on a spit. The Red Captain screamed with some eldritch, unholy, echoing roar, and the energies of his conjuration convulsed and sputtered. He did not bend, or go limp, but he slowly, with dreadful menace, brought his gaze to Mars Gulgynn.

Aras reached out with one burnt hand, grasping the three-handed hilt of Ruin. In his grip, Mars' hand bones turned to pulp, and he fell to one side. The blade was still planted wholly in the wizard's chest, and time seemed to stop.

Then, with slow motion and the abject horror of evil unimagined, he drew the blade out. Hand over hand on the endless blade he worked. The steel was sheathed with an even, glistening crimson coat. At last, as all those still alive were transfixed with shock, the blade was revealed and lifted. It was stained red, but a bright, hellish red all folding in swirls and spirals. It was no longer Ruin. This blade was forged in the belly of a demon, and drawn forth to end the world. Red Fang was it called from that day forward.

But the names and history of great swords is the province of historians, and those brave warriors still breathing wasted not a single gasp in the awe of it all.

Before Akram, now leaping like a lion, could reach the wizard, Mars had regained his wits. His hands were purple mush, but his valor was still untarnished. The Red Captain's rapture of power had distracted him, and there was a tiny window of opportunity. Mars thought not of himself, or of fear, or of agony. He braced both boots behind him, then rose from his knees. All the might of his thighs he brought to bear, pushing like an elephant. With arms and elbows, he tangled the Red Captain in a clumsy grapple, and the villainous wizard pitched backward, nothing to stop his fall.

Into the yawning abyss they tumbled; Red Fang, and Aras of Iridess, and Mars Gulgynn, the hero of Fort Friendship. The Red Captain howled, and the clanging of Mars' armor echoed down, down, down into the unknowable fathoms of the deep.

So it ended.

So it ended, there in the eyes of Hela the Goddess of Mirth and Truth. So met their deaths the heroes of that time. So grief and endless woe did Hannar, Hunnin's son find. He could not be consoled, or comforted, and he wailed and wept at his mother's side in that lonely cavern. He rocked back and forth with a horrible sadness, and held her. There was no shield, no quest, no heroic trumpets for victory earned. Only the crushing weight of wrath's futile fury.

So it ended.

So it began.

24

In time, Elisa, Akram, Hannar, and Kray, now the last of the Elite, made their way to the roads of Duros. There they met friends of the King, and on wooden wheels made their way eventually homeward. They were beaten, bloody, and exhausted. Grief lay on their faces like a shadow. It was a dark day for victory. To Ramthas they bumped and jostled.

Hannar said nothing, and stared into the sky in catatonic confusion.

Monuments were raised for their return, and preparations made for war. Vows were sworn and bonds made that would endure forever.

Kray and Elisa's love was cemented by their ordeal. Even as she towered over him, a hero for all to behold, he stood straight and tall. Theirs was a love made in crisis, and would outlast the very stars. They were married before the War of the Wall broke.

Hannar came of age, and was the first of the Anvil Knights. What cruel irony that he would be the last. He grew to be a man of few words and dire strength. Not easily could his victories be counted, but he never knew glory's celebration. His was a life of darkness and memories fading. Too young had he met death, and the glint of evil in Aras' spell never fully left the back of his mind. Always the Devourer was there, waiting in dreams, and it made him fierce as a lion.

At Akram's side were these few always, along with Lawgiver, Angrid the ancient sword, or Huro Din as called by the dwarves.

"We will never forget," Akram's great kingly voice rang out to all Ramthas at the memorial this and every year hence, "for our peace is blood-won by sacrifice. Look to your left; there stands your shield. In each other we place our faith, and in every action, we earn this trust. Ours is a strength as old as the Greenway, and immovable as the sun."

Elisa placed a mighty hand on Hannar's shoulder. He was gleaming in ceremonial plate in those days. She was immaculate, towering, muscled like a warhorse and beautiful as a goddess.

"She was a great warrior... A true shieldmaiden. No defeat will tarnish her valor, old friend."

Hannar did not answer. Among rows of Anvil Knights, he prowled and scowled, memories of his mother and father etched in his brows. And it was he who brought up the greatest fighting force that ever walked Alfheim.

Now you know how it began; how the War of the Wall found its roots in a mother's scream for her child. How those lonely heroes met doom head-on in the depths of the earth. How the power called Red Fang came into this world, and how Mars Gulgynn met his end a hero.

As the war eventually unfolded, the Red Captain somehow arose from his doom in the pits, Red Fang on his belt. No longer mortal was he then, but a demon from hell returned worse than ever. Mars' victory was sealed though, for the delay of the Red resurrection ensured Ramthas was prepared, the Wall lined with pikes, and those ready to die for righteousness beyond the counting.

Atop the Wall of Duros they fought Red Fang, where once Hannar had defied him single-handed. Legions of elven warriors crashed like waves on a rock in the cataclysmic battles of that war, and the good folk of Alfheim stood firm against the hordes, fending off the eyeless, twisting whips and tentacles of that unholy army.

But that is another story.

Made in the USA
San Bernardino, CA
12 June 2017